# A Dangerous King

## BOOK FOUR

### The Sentinels

# J. S. SCOTT

A Dangerous King
The Sentinels: Book Four

Copyright © 2016 by J. S. Scott

Cover Design by Stacey Chappell

ISBN: 978-1-7930-7664-9

# AUTHOR NOTE

I'd like to thank every reader who has read my Sentinel Series. It's never been my most popular series, but I've loved every moment that I've spent in their world, and I feel both happy and sad that this is their last story.

For everyone who loved the way my Sentinels love their *radiants*—not with their eyes, but with their soul—this last story, where every Sentinel finally has a HEA… this story is for you.

# Author Acknowledgments

As usual, thank you to all of my KA team: Sri, Sandie, Tami, Natalie, Isa and Annette. I know I'm biased, but I think I have the best support team an author could ever have.

Thank you to all of the Gems for your continued support. Best. Street. Team. Ever.

Special thanks to Natalie for the amazing cover for this book. He is so Kristoff!

Lastly, thanks so much to Alicia, who proofed this book on very short notice.

You all rock!

XXX ~ Jan (J.S. Scott)

# Contents

# Prologue

"*The Sentinels—A History*"
*AUTHOR—DR. TALIA MARIS-WINSTON, PHD.*

*M*any people believe that demons are evil spirits, possessing humans, taking over their minds and bodies until they are nothing but a shell, a vessel for the evil entity that dwells inside them. What most humans don't know is that there are also other types of demons, physical beings created thousands of years ago, during a period of time when demons came to rule the Earth, having been set loose by careless gods who used them for chaos and revenge. The gods created them in so great a number that they finally had to confine all their creations to a demon realm, a prison that could contain them. Said gods, who are now considered nothing more than myth, and whose vanity was endless, adamantly refused to destroy the demons—to annihilate all of them would be an admission that what the deities had done was actually wrong. All-powerful, all-knowing gods and demigods did not make errors. They themselves declared it impossible. And how could they destroy their own magic, lose creatures that might be needed later? After all, the gods were usually at war, and what if they needed their *evil creations for weapons? So instead, the demons stayed confined to the demon realm, a place where no god would venture—a realm of such vile evilness, such toxicity and so malodorous, that no selfish deity could tolerate visiting.*

*The realm was hidden, situated between Earth and Hades, a place where the demons remained, multiplied, and grew in strength while the gods ignored their existence. Unfortunately, ignoring such heinous immortals eventually created utter chaos, the demons finally gaining enough power to leave the demon realm and create havoc on an Earth that was, by that time, inhabited by a large population of humans. These demons became known as the Evils.*

*Devastation ruled, human beings taken in large numbers, disappearing in droves. The balance between good and evil tipped, evil ruling the planet, creating a rift that not even the gods themselves could fix. Desperate to restore sanity to an insane world, the gods tried in vain to destroy the vile beasts that upset the equilibrium, finally putting aside their vanity in favor of survival. But it was too late; the demon population was too large, too powerful, and the egotistic gods weren't about to venture near the Evils to destroy them.*

*Desperate, the deities banded together and created a new breed of demon to fight the Evils; the newcomers' souls would still be dark, but their purpose would be to protect humans from becoming extinct, bringing good and evil back into balance. These newly-created Sentinel demons blended in, appearing human…but they weren't. They were magical beings, although they adapted and took on more facets of humanity as they evolved. Having given the guardian demons the power to recruit humans and thus replace Sentinels lost in the battle between good and evil, the gods no longer needed to be bothered with their "annoying little problem" and went to war with each other once again, losing power as the centuries passed and humans ceased to worship them. However, the Sentinels carried on, striving to protect the human population, governing themselves and growing in magical powers, even though the gods had embedded a set of rules into the Sentinels' magic— supposed fail-safes imposed to keep the guardian demons in check. Still, the Sentinels brought balance back to the planet in spite of the stifling* rules, finding ways to bend them or work around them, angry that the only rule imposed on the Evils was that human victims could not initially be taken by force, or coerced via lies. But manipulation was easy for an Evil, and once a human had agreed to an Evil's bargain, there was no end to the torture the heinous demons could impose upon the duped individual in order to increase their own strength.

So…are all demons evil? They are all dark at their core, and have some degree of inherent wickedness…but demons were not all created equal.

Evils and Sentinels are both demons, engaging to this day in a battle of good versus evil that has been going on for thousands of years, a war that most humans are blissfully unaware even exists. However, for the small percentage of individuals who actually have encounters with demons…their lives will never be the same.

# Chapter One

*H*e only heard her when he was trying *not* to sleep.

Quite honestly, here in the demon realm, he was pretty much *always* trying not to slip into slumber because it would only make his misery worse. He didn't need much sleep, but the deprivation was getting to him now, sending him closer to the edge of insanity. Eventually, he wouldn't be able to avoid sleeping, and the Evils would take what was left of his reason.

Unless he heard *her* voice.

Kristoff Agares, King of the Sentinel Demons, wanted nothing more than to hear the sweet voice that lulled him into a healing sleep when he was actually conscious enough to respond to her instructions to sleep undisturbed. Lately, he wasn't hearing her at all, and that meant letting the Evils enter his dreams, and they conjured up nightmares that were seriously screwing up his mind.

How long had he been trapped in the Evil's demon Hell?

*A day?*

*A week?*

*Years?*

Strangely, he was more than concerned about the woman with the mystery voice. Where was she? Was she safe?

It was hard to know exactly what length of time he'd been here, shackled and tortured in every imaginable way. The demon realm ran on a different time, and varied enormously from the human world. Because he was being held captive and subjected to nearly every kind of anguish, he could well believe he'd been in Goran's prison for eons, but it had probably only been a matter of days in the human realm.

In reality, he really *didn't* know. He was considerably weakened, and it was getting difficult to separate reality from delusion.

And dammit...he was pissed off! He'd sworn to himself that when Athena had created him as the first and the king of the Sentinels, he'd never be in a vulnerable position again. He'd fucking had enough of that in his life before he'd become the Sentinel king. When the goddess had given him such a grave responsibility, he'd vowed always to put his men and the human world first. Since then, he'd had a purpose, a responsibility that he had been more than willing to take on with a vengeance.

Now, all he wanted was to see Goran pay for messing with anybody Kristoff was responsible for protecting.

He wanted revenge on the Evils' leader for having no honor, and for the pain and suffering he'd brought to Kristoff's Sentinels and the human world he was sworn to protect.

His burning desire to protect all of them, to not give up on the people he cared about, was about the only thing that kept Kristoff from giving up.

*I can't sleep. I can't sleep.*

He was exhausted, but the only time he dared give in and close his eyes was when he heard the voice of what appeared to be a guardian of his slumber. There were no invasions into his dreams when she spoke to him. Sadly, she didn't speak often, or else he was getting too weak to hear her words.

Awkwardly, Kristoff tried desperately to sit up, but his chains wouldn't allow it. There was only enough length to keep his arms stretched out to his side, and his legs straight. His clothing had been taken long ago, but he could smell the stench of his own body, and the nauseating smell of rotting flesh that had been torn off him piece by piece.

*I'm a demigod, the leader of the Sentinel Demons, and I can't even clean myself up.*

His head slammed back onto the steel frame he was resting on with disgust, giving up the futile attempt to move. His magic was long gone, obliterated in this realm. It pissed him off to no end that the entire world was in turmoil, and the Sentinels were going to lose the fight between good and evil. Even here in the demon realm, Kristoff could feel the tipping point coming, the inevitable shift that would put the balance in the Evils' favor—the point of no return. Once that happened, there would be no way for the Sentinels to make things even again. The human realm would be overrun by the Evils, and his Sentinels would perish one by one, until all of them were gone.

*I should be there. I should at least be able to lead the fight, even if we're destined to lose. I should be the first one to lose my head—literally—in battle.*

But what choice had he been given?

Leave his newfound daughter, Talia, to the Evils' mercy? *Nope.* Goran and his demons would have destroyed his innocent daughter in a matter of minutes. Drew might have hung on a little longer, but if Talia had perished, Drew would have welcomed death. Kristoff hadn't been able to do that. Besides, Talia would have been needed, not only by her mate, Drew, but by the entire world. With her latent power now exposed, the Sentinels needed every special *radiant* they could get on their side.

*We just don't have enough strength.*

The Evils had grown in power over the centuries, using unsuspecting humans and undiscovered *radiants* to amass a nearly unstoppable force that the Sentinels had been unable to equal.

*Because we fucking stick to the rules. The Evils are no longer bound to their creator.*

Kristoff despised the ingrained part of his soul that insisted he honor the laws that had been set during the beginning of the war between the Evils and the Sentinels in ancient times. Because his creator, the goddess Athena, was still alive and dwelled on Earth, he was unwillingly forced to follow those rules. He couldn't do otherwise. The gods who had created the Evils were long gone, so the bastards had stopped following the dictates of the gods centuries ago.

*Athena?*

Kristoff reached out to his maker with his mind, even though he knew trying to contact her was useless. His powers were gone, and there was no reaching out mentally to anybody while he was here in the demon realm. He had no idea how the mysteriously soothing female voice had occasionally penetrated his mind, lulled him to sleep without nightmares. For all he knew, *she* could be a hallucination. Maybe he had been hearing what he wanted to hear. Maybe it was all just the Evils fucking with his head.

*Why won't you talk to me?*

He mentally bellowed out his need to hear a voice that wasn't an Evil, a tone that was kind and gentle.

There was no answer.

Kristoff retreated into himself, his body shaking with pain, anger and remorse.

There was no reprieve for him. In truth, there never had been.

Her name was Sophie.

Really, that was nearly all she knew about herself. Captured and brought to the demon realm at a young age, she remembered none of the details of her childhood, nothing before she'd lived here as a slave to Goran and the Evils.

She'd grown up here in demon Hell, but for some reason her appearance had changed very little once she'd reached maturity. Sophie had no idea how long she'd been in this realm of torment, destruction and death, but it was way longer than it took for a body to grow old and die. That fact was no comfort to her. Really, eternal life here in the demon realm was the ultimate torture for her. She would have rather grown old and finally found some peace in death.

Rising from the blanket on the filthy floor, Sophie tried to slowly stand up, looking around for the other *radiants*, and realizing that they were all gone.

*Again!*

A shudder ran through her body, knowing she should be used to finding herself alone in the area of the demon realm where the *radiants* were held.

The cycle had gone on for what seemed like forever. *Radiants* came in one by one, and she made friends with them, learning about the human world from the women who had been caught just like she had. Then, Goran would arrive, sucking the power from all of them, leaving her to wake alone God-knew-how-long later. Time meant little in the demon realm. There was no real day or night, no real passing of time. It was always dark, always vile, always the same.

The *radiants* who were brought here had told her about the human world, the place where she *really* belonged. It was a life she couldn't even remember. The other *radiants* had all been horrified by the Hell they'd been confined in, but Sophie didn't really understand the difference. It was the only life she'd ever known.

*It's good to know there's something better out there somewhere, even if I can only remember it through the human women who passed through this realm.*

She didn't wonder what had happened to the other women that had been here before Goran had sucked the power from her body. Sophie had long ago managed not to ponder their fate. From listening to the other demons speak, she knew that she was always the sole survivor of the power sucks that Goran did on a regular basis. So many women had come and gone that Sophie had to close down her emotions, bury them so deeply that they never escaped. If she thought about the fate of those other females, she'd never stay sane through the constant grief of knowing that none of them had lived through Goran's torment except her.

*Why me?*

Every time Goran drained her until she became unconscious, she *wished* that it would be the time she wouldn't wake up. Unfortunately, she'd survived every incident for so long that she kept becoming more and more detached when she realized the other women were gone.

*Dead. They all die except me.*

When she started to feel the remorse rise, she pushed it back down.

*Never show them that you're scared, that the Evils can affect you in any way.*

Her reaction had been ingrained into her early, after she realized that the more fear and anger she showed, the more the Evils liked to torment her. Eventually, she'd learned to recognize every venomous word they said. Sometimes she wished she'd stayed ignorant, but when the ancient demon language was all she ever heard when there weren't new female victims present, one started to understand the demon language.

She walked slowly to the corner of the room, finding the meager amount of food and water that had been left for her. The stale bread went down reluctantly with the cup of water left on the ground. It was her usual allowance of sustenance. For some reason, they fed her. Granted, the bread was in short supply as was the liquid she needed to continue to function. But Goran wanted her alive, and Sophie had finally realized that she existed only so he could continue to suck power from her body.

As she chewed the hard crust, she vaguely wondered about who her mate should have been. Was he dead, or was he still alive and fighting what the Evils swore was a losing fight on Earth?

Sophie knew what she was, that she was meant to be the human mate of a Sentinel demon. She'd been in the demon realm long enough to learn and understand the truth. Sometimes Goran tried to use the information to upset her—not that he succeeded anymore. She showed no emotion, reacted to nothing any of the Evils said. But she listened, and she knew what her fate *should* have been. Stuck in the depths of Hell, it was hard not to occasionally wonder what her life might have been like if she hadn't been taken from the human realm.

*Why won't you talk to me?*

Sophie startled as the low, tormented voice sounded in her mind. *Kristoff. The Sentinel Demon King.*

Before she'd been drained by Goran, she'd been able to reach out to him, connect to him with a telepathic communication line that she'd never experienced before.

*Ever since I sneaked into the dungeon and spoke to him.*

Sophie was allowed to wander through the demon realm. There was nowhere to go and no way for her to escape. As long as she kept quiet and did what the demons wanted—Goran in particular—they didn't bother to confine her anymore.

Usually, she rarely left the area where she slept, but when she'd heard that the Sentinel Demon King was Goran's prisoner, Sophie had wanted and needed to see him. The compulsion had been so strong; she hadn't been able to fight it. Risking punishment if she was caught, she'd snuck into the dungeon, the one place where she knew she couldn't wander. Especially when prisoners were being held.

Kristoff's appearance had shocked her. Although she'd seen human women, he was the first male she remembered seeing who appeared to be human. Sure, he was actually a Sentinel demon and a demigod, but from what she'd heard, most Sentinels were once human, and they stayed in the same physical form after they became a Sentinel.

Even confused, Kristoff had been so handsome, so different from the male Evils. It had been a shock when she'd realized that she could hear his thoughts, and that she could speak to him in her mind. Following her instincts, she'd followed him into his dreams, and been able to block his usual nightmares, let him sleep a dreamless sleep.

She'd had to leave him or risk discovery. There was no way for her to free him. But after the visit, Sophie had tried to protect him every chance she had. Unfortunately, she'd been out of it for a while because Goran had drained her, and she wasn't even certain how long she'd been unconscious.

*I'm here. I'm sorry. My energy was taken from me. But I'm back now.*
Sophie sent the message through the channel that she knew instinctively only she and Kristoff shared.

There was silence for a moment before he answered.

*You were drained? Are you one of the captive radiants? Are you here in the demon realm?*

He sounded lost and confused. Sophie's heart ached for the pain he'd been through, and it was one of the only emotions she'd let touch her in a very long time.

*Yes. I'm the only one who ever survives for very long. I don't know why.*
He answered quicker this time.

*I know why. You're a special radiant, one with a latent power. Are you alone now?*

She nodded sadly and swallowed hard, even though she knew Kristoff couldn't see her.

*Yes. The other women are all...gone.*
His answer came back stronger.

*Fuck! Damn Goran to Hell!*
She replied drily.

*He's already in demon Hell.*
Kristoff was quiet for a moment before he answered with a slightly amused reply.

*Are you really here, or am I so damn lost to reality that I'm hallucinating?*

Sophie knew what the demons were capable of, and she knew they wanted Kristoff as weak and as close to dead as he could possibly get. He was a powerful Sentinel, the king with the powers of a demigod, and he was a threat unless he was totally incapacitated.

However, having the Sentinel king was a valuable asset to the Evils until they totally won the wars that was going on in the human realm. With no leader, no demigod to help them, the Sentinels were bound to lose their fight.

*I'm real, Kristoff. The room where I stay lies just above you. I visited you briefly, but you were exhausted. You didn't know I was there. For some reason, I can speak to you now telepathically. I can guard you from some of the mental torment the demons are bombarding you with. But once I was drained by Goran, I was unconscious. I don't know how long I was out. I'm sorry I left you.*

He sent his next message quickly.

*It's not your fault. How long have you been here?*

Sophie shuddered as she replied.

*Forever. I don't remember my life in the human realm. All I know is what I've been able to overhear from the demons and from the poor radiants who are brought here to die.*

His tone was gruff as he sent a reply.

*Don't. Don't feel responsible. You're a prisoner just like they were. I wish there was some way for me to get the hell out of here and help my Sentinels.*

The fact that he appeared to want out of the demon realm just to help his men with the battle didn't escape her notice.

"But the other women always die and I don't," Sophie muttered to herself, unwilling to put anything more on Kristoff by sending the words telepathically.

She wanted him to live.

She wanted him to escape.

She wanted him to get back to where he belonged so the Sentinels had a chance to win against the Evils.

Sophie might not remember the human realm, but she did know it had to be a hell of a lot nicer than the demon's domain. Evil was evil. The Sentinels were the good guys. Somehow, Kristoff had to live and return to his own dimension.

Here, he was helpless.

*Tell me what I can do to help you.*

Her request was desperate. She didn't have enough knowledge to know exactly how she could return him to his own world.

*Nothing. I traded my life for my daughter and her mate. Even if I had the power to leave, I can't. I sealed my fate. I gave my vow.*

The frustration in Kristoff's voice was clear, but Sophie didn't have much time to think about his words before all hell broke loose.

All Sophie could do was gape as a beautiful woman with flame-colored hair appeared out of thin air, followed by a female with dark hair, and then another behind her. The last one was a woman with hair a similar color to Kristoff's, a light, gorgeous blonde with a ferocious expression that brought Sophie to a halt as she started walking toward them.

*There are no Evils accompanying them into the demon realm!*

These women weren't new arrivals for Goran to drain. They were here by choice for some reason, able to descend into the realm without the help of the Evils, and judging from the blonde woman's expression, they were obviously pretty damn angry.

Sophie could sense that these women were *radiants*, but they were unlike any other Sentinel demon mate she'd ever encountered.

*Because they're already mated!*

Sophie could feel the difference. These women exuded more confidence and power than the unclaimed *radiants*, yet they still had the same essence as the women who had perished here in the demon realm.

They were *radiants*, but definitely not alone and not undefended like the *radiants* who came here and died here.

Sentinel demons followed one by one, the dark-haired female touching each one of them, which seemed to make them come alive with energy. Every male and the blonde female manifested a very wicked-looking sword, turning just in time to engage the swarm of Evils that came running from the hallway and into the large cavern.

Every Sentinel was formidable, easily divesting the lesser Evils of their heads, sometimes slaying several with one powerful swing of their weapons. Their numbers were small, but their determination and courage seemed endless.

Sophie watched, her heart in her throat, silently hoping that the Sentinels would be victorious. She didn't have any sympathy for the dying Evils. They'd been tormenting her forever, and had killed more human females than she could count. Honestly, she was hoping that all of the Evils' victims would be avenged. It wouldn't bring them back, but they deserved champions to slay the Evils that had murdered them.

"I need to find Kristoff," the blonde woman yelled in order to be heard among the chaos.

"Go. We can handle this," one of the dark-haired men growled loudly. "We'll find Goran and have him here for you when you return."

Sophie didn't miss the quick look the fierce man sent to the female who had said she needed to find Kristoff. It was an expression that promised if she wasn't back soon, he'd be coming for her.

*Were they mated?* Sophie couldn't say for sure, but the protective look on the Sentinel's face pretty much spoke volumes.

Propelling herself forward, Sophie quickly approached the angelic-looking woman who was making her way to the exit of the large room in her quest to find Kristoff. Evils were still advancing, but the male Sentinels were holding their own.

"I know where Kristoff is being held," Sophie told the woman breathlessly. "I'll take you there."

Sophie found herself under close scrutiny as she was examined by the intelligent blue-eyed gaze of the dainty angel who was still wearing a murderous expression.

"Interesting," the woman rasped, turning her attention to mowing down more Evils. "Where is he?"

"We have to get through this hallway and down to the dungeon," Sophie instructed, following close behind the woman and her sword. "He's being held right beneath this room."

"You're one of the special *radiants*. What's your name, child?"

Sophie wasn't special in any way, and she didn't understand the woman's comment, but she kept following the mesmerizing blonde, convinced that *this* was Kristoff's rescue team. His chance to get free and return to the human realm.

By now, the dirt floor was piling up with the remains of the demons who were quickly meeting their demise and turning from goo to ash. Sophie just continued to plow through it, feeling nothing but relief as each Evil fell. Whoever this earthly female was, she wasn't anything like the others who had died. In fact, her strength was almost palpable.

"I'm Sophie, and I haven't been a child for a very long time." She'd grown up here in the demon realm, and although she hadn't aged much once she'd reached adulthood, she was far from young, and she definitely wasn't innocent. "Who are *you*?" she asked hurriedly as she reached the door of the dungeon, turned the large metal key and yanked to get it open.

"I'm Athena. Even though you're an adult now, I assure you I'm old enough to call you a child," she answered with certainty. "Do you already know you belong to Kristoff?"

"I belong to no one," Sophie shot back at her angrily. "I might be a prisoner, but nobody will own me."

Athena ducked through the door as soon as there was a lull of oncoming Evils and followed Sophie down the black, concrete stairs.

"How did you know he was here?" Athena asked as she followed close behind Sophie's rapid movement.

"We…communicate. I know it sounds strange, but we can actually mind-speak."

"Not so weird since you have a rather important connection. Unusual perhaps, and it hasn't happened this way in the past. But

Kristoff is…different," Athena answered. "It's hard to tell how his mating experience will differ from other Sentinels since he's a demigod, the first of his kind, and the king."

*Mating experience? Had Kristoff found his mate only to be torn away from her and into the demon realm?*

Sophie didn't understand much of what Athena was saying, so she focused more on finding and rescuing Kristoff. For some reason, it was critical to her that he lived and got back to the human realm where he belonged.

"This way," Sophie instructed as she led Athena down a dark hallway once they reached the bottom of the stairs.

Athena made short work of the guards, lopping off their ugly heads, hardly hesitating in her determination to get to the demon king.

Sophie sent Kristoff a mental message so he wasn't taken by surprise.

*I'm with a woman named Athena. We're coming to release you.*

Sophie's steps faltered as Kristoff roared.

*She's not a woman. She's a goddamn goddess. What in the hell is she doing here? Is she alone? Dammit! The last thing I want is for her to die on a suicide mission.*

Athena was a goddess? No wonder she was kicking ass against the lesser Evils.

*She isn't alone. I'm showing her where you are, and your Sentinels are doing battle with the Evils.*

Pointing Athena down another dark tunnel, the goddess turned left as instructed.

*Goddammit! They can't be here. The toxins will kill them, and they have no powers. They'll all be slaughtered.*

While most people would be relieved that rescue was in sight, Kristoff sounded angry that anybody had risked their life for him. Sophie thought it was admirable that he'd rather die than see any of his Sentinels and friends perish. She answered as she reached his cell, "They seem to be doing just fine," she spoke aloud, getting her first glimpse of Kristoff since soon after he'd arrived.

The punishment he'd taken made Sophie sick to her stomach.

"Oh, gods!" Athena exclaimed with alarm, raising her hand to the bars of the cell. "You don't look good, Kristoff. We need to get you out of here quickly."

The supposedly impenetrable cage disintegrated at the will of the goddess.

"What are you doing here, Athena? How in the hell did you leave your mansion?" Kristoff asked angrily, but the weakness in his voice spoke of how depleted he was in his current state.

Sophie bit back a gasp as she saw that his face was now nearly unrecognizable, the blood and injuries making his features distorted and disguised. Flesh had been torn from the rest of his body, and the cell floor was running red with Kristoff's blood.

Looking like she was concentrating as she broke each shackle on his limbs, Athena answered sharply, "You should be glad I'm here. You weren't going to last much longer. Luckily, it appears that you had your *radiant* here to keep you from completely losing your mind." As Kristoff tried to sit up, Athena ordered, "Don't try to move. I'm sending you and Sophie back to your home. I know she'll watch over you. I need to confront Goran and strip him of his stolen power. I don't have time to explain right now, but we'll fill you in when we get back."

Sophie flinched when Athena put one hand on top of her head, and the other on Kristoff's. Giving her a stern look, the goddess demanded, "Take care of him. We'll follow you shortly."

Sophie felt her whole world tilt on its axis before she could reply, the spinning dizziness turning into a darkness that consumed her until she was no longer able to think or reason, the blackness surrounding her and swallowing her whole.

The first thing Sophie noticed when she woke was that wherever Kristoff lived, it smelled a whole lot better than the demon realm. Looking around, still dazed, she was momentarily awed by how clean the enormous room was, and how there wasn't a single pile of bones and refuse in sight.

It had to be some kind of sitting room, with chairs and sofas directed toward a big black screen. The floor they'd landed on was covered in plush fabric.

"Kristoff?" He was right next to her, and he appeared to be out cold.

The goddess must have somehow fixed most of his injuries. He was lying on his back, naked, his flesh returned to his body and his features normal again.

"God, you're so handsome," Sophie mused as she cupped his cheek, noticing he was cool to the touch. Running her hand down his chest, she discovered he was cold everywhere. When she reached the bottom of his stomach, she stopped, her face red with embarrassment as she stared at his male member. Part of her wanted to touch it, but she didn't want to violate Kristoff when he wasn't aware.

Standing up slowly, she felt a little bit dizzy, but otherwise normal. She shook off her lightheadedness, her focus on Kristoff's cold body.

"He needs to get warm," she mumbled to herself, watching the regular rise and fall of his breathing. He was obviously not in any distress, but maybe he needed a period of healing sleep.

Glancing across the enormous room, she spotted a door leading into another area of his house, and she started toward it, determined to find something to cover Kristoff, a blanket or two if she could locate where he kept them.

Slipping out the door, she hesitated as she took in the grand surroundings. Twinkling chandeliers hung high from the hand-painted ceilings, and all of the fixtures appeared to be gold. Still, she vaguely observed that the mansion was startlingly masculine and classic without being gaudy. Taking the stairs to her right, she gaped at the lavish furnishings as she walked into room after room of the upper level, grabbing covers from a few of the beds before sprinting back down the flight of steps again.

*What did I expect? He's the Sentinel King. Of course he has an impressive home.*

The large house just seemed so temptingly inviting, and so clean. Where the demon realm was dark and ugly, the human realm was light and colorful, so bright it almost hurt her eyes.

Kneeling next to Kristoff, she covered him with the blankets she'd found and sat next to him to keep watch. His skin was still cool, but was it just a little bit warmer than it had been—or was it just wishful thinking?

Part of her desperately wanted him to open his eyes, look at her without the cover of darkness to hide her. But there was some relief that he hadn't seen her face yet.

*He's so beautiful, so perfect.*

*And I'm…not.*

Would he flinch with horror when he saw her in the light of the human daytime?

More than likely, he would. Most of the human female *radiants* had looked at her in sympathy, but a few had blatantly avoided her because of the way she looked. Sophie had gotten to the point where she ignored the women who were afraid of her physical appearance, even though she'd assured them she wasn't contagious and hadn't been for a very long time.

However, for some reason, Kristoff's reaction *would* matter to her. She couldn't quite figure out why since she hardly knew him.

Remembering what the goddess had said about belonging to Kristoff, she wondered what exactly Athena had meant. How could she belong to him unless…?

The goddess had said something about Kristoff's mating experience, but all of Sophie's focus had been on the danger they were facing, and her urgency to save Kristoff.

"Was she possibly trying to hint that *I'm* his *radiant?*" she wondered aloud. "There's no way *that's* possible."

Kristoff was strong, powerful and wise. He was also physically perfect in every way. He'd have a beauty for a mate, probably a female who looked like Athena.

*But we did have that strange path of mental communication. Could that be because…?*

No!

She couldn't even think about the possibility of being Kristoff's *radiant*. Obviously she'd been meant for *someone*, but it couldn't be the Sentinel king. Why would he end up with a hideously scarred woman who wasn't even familiar with the modern human world? What kind of support could she ever provide him as his mate?

*I wouldn't be an asset; more like a liability.*

Sophie jumped as the goddess took shape right beside her, followed by the two other women who had come with her to the Evils' dimension, and three of the Sentinels Sophie had seen slaying a whole lot of demons.

"How is he?" one of the dark-haired men asked, kneeling beside her in concern, even though he looked worn out and injured himself.

"Healed by the goddess, but not conscious for some reason," Sophie replied, looking up to meet the eyes of the worried Sentinel. "His skin is cold. I covered him, but I didn't know what else to do." *Maybe because I know almost nothing about healing a Sentinel, or a human for that matter.*

The goddess instantly healed any wounds on the men, and then turned to the women, touching each of them as she explained, "I need to make sure none of you are going to get sick from demon realm toxins. Kristoff is still out because I couldn't totally clear them from his body. He broke a promise, and even though I did what I could, he'll suffer a little for a while. There's nothing I can do."

Sophie was still looking at the Sentinel beside her. His eyes were glued to hers, and although she didn't see any disgust in his expression, she immediately assumed he was staring at her horrible appearance in the stark light of day.

*It's going to be far worse here. There's so much...light.*

She found herself fighting the instinct to turn her face away. If she was going to dwell among the humans, she was going to have to get used to them staring.

Athena waved her hand. "I'm sending Kristoff to his bed. We can watch over him there. I think he's been uncomfortable for long enough."

"I'll go up and sit with him," the other two women said in unison, both of them bolting for the steps.

"Sophie?" The man kneeling beside her finally spoke, his voice low and filled with shock and awe.

"Yes? How did you know my name?" Did the goddess tell them? Certainly she'd been a bit too busy for that.

"Sophie. Jesus, I can't believe you're here. How are you alive?" he asked hoarsely, his tone clearly astonished.

"You know me?" She suddenly recognized that she had some strange connection to this man. She felt it, and her heart started to hammer against the wall of her chest. His features were somehow dear and so familiar, yet she couldn't place exactly *how* she knew him.

He grasped her shoulders and shook her lightly. "Sophie, it's Zach. Of course I remember you. You might be older and all grown up, but your features are still the same. You look like me. You always did. I thought you were dead. I thought you died of smallpox when you were a child. This is so fucking unbelievable that I'm almost afraid it's not true. But I know it is," he said hoarsely as he looked at her with adoration in his eyes.

His expression, so ravaged and yet so hopeful, rendered Sophie almost speechless. "What is true?" she whispered, her heart still galloping as she stared into a pair of dark eyes so much like her own.

"I've mourned your loss for so long that I'm afraid to believe it's really you. But I know you're my Sophie. Not only can I see it, but I feel it. Sophie, it's me. Zach. I'm your brother."

# Chapter Three

ach wasn't sure what to do. Everything inside him wanted to reach out and grab the baby sister he'd thought was gone from him forever, then hug her until she couldn't breathe. But something was wrong. Something was...off.

He knew without a doubt that this was his only sibling, his baby sister who had died the day he'd become a Sentinel. So how was it possible she was here now?

*I'm not going to question a miracle, even if I don't completely understand. There's only one thing I really want right now.*

"Can I hug you?" he asked, holding his breath. She obviously didn't remember him. *Strange.* She'd been young when she'd supposedly died, but old enough that she should have *some* memories.

Sophie nodded slowly like she was in a daze, so Zach was careful, slowly gathering her thin, fragile body against him, his eyes damp as he cradled his precious little sister. He'd gone through her loss, grieved for her. Really, the sorrow had never gone away. To this day, even after over two centuries, he mourned her loss. He'd never gotten over the pain of causing her death, not being there with her when she'd died.

"Zach," she said tremulously, and then started to sob against his shoulder.

"You're remembering?" he asked hesitantly. There had been a little recognition and awareness in her voice.

"Little things are coming back to me...like working together in London, trying to survive. I'm not sure if being in the demon realm blocked my memories, or if I did it myself. It was so long ago, but I remember now how much I missed you. I'm not sure how I ever forgot you." She put her arms around his neck and hugged him back.

Zach released a sigh of relief. He wasn't sure why Sophie had lost her memories, but he was willing to bet they'd been stolen by the Evils to keep her lost and confused. Once outside of the demon realm, it made sense that they'd return.

"I'm so damn sorry, Soph," he said hoarsely. "I've always hated myself for not being there when you died." He hesitated before correcting himself, "But I guess you didn't really die." Hell, he didn't know what to say. Just the fact that Sophie was still alive seemed surreal. Reluctantly, he let her go and pulled her to her feet so he could seat them both on the sofa.

"This is your sister?" Drew asked, sitting in one of the chairs as Hunter did the same.

"Yes," Zach answered proudly, still in awe because Sophie was sitting right beside him. "Sophie, this is Hunter and Drew, the other Winston brothers."

He took a few minutes to explain what had happened to him after he'd found her sickbed empty, assuming she'd already been buried in a mass grave. Sophie asked a few questions, but she mostly listened. He noted that although she'd physically changed, she still got the same contemplative look on her face when she was processing information.

"You didn't die?" Hunter finally asked, sounding curious about what had happened to Sophie.

She shook her head. "No. I was taken by the Evils."

"You made a deal," Zach guessed.

The room went silent, and he was fairly certain that his sister didn't want to admit that she'd sacrificed her own life to keep him from dying. In fact, she'd been so worried about him that she hadn't cared what happened to her in the process.

Finally, Sophie looked at Zach. "I wanted you to live. I didn't want you to get sick. I foolishly agreed to go with the Evils if they'd let you stay safe, well, and healthy. I admit that I wasn't totally aware of what was happening or who the Evils really were. My fever was so high that my thoughts were muddled, but I knew I wanted you to be okay. I knew I was going to die from the smallpox, Zach. My fate was already sealed."

Zach's eyes clouded over. "But you might not have—"

"Don't, Zach," Sophie pleaded, cutting her brother off. "Even though I was a child, I knew I was going to die. I sensed it."

He let out a masculine sigh as Sophie put a gentle palm on his cheek, comforting him. His sister was trying to make him feel better, even though he'd screwed up so long ago. He reached up and curled his fingers around her hand. "I can't believe you're here. You're alive."

"It was always meant to be this way, Zach." He heard Athena's voice behind him, making him realize she must have popped back into the room. "Had she not gone with the Evils, she would have died."

"Then fate sucks," he grumbled as he slowly released Sophie's hand. "Why did it have to be so hard for her?"

"Because she's Kristoff's fated mate," Athena replied, meeting his stare when he stood up and faced her. "It wasn't her time to leave the Earth, but it also wasn't their time to be mated. She was still a child."

"So she was committed to what had to have been like an eternity in the demon realm," Zach angrily shot back at the goddess.

"Would you have gone through anything in order to be with Kat?"

Kat was everything to Zach, and there's nothing he wouldn't do, nothing he'd regret if that was what it had taken to be with her. He would have spent thousands of years in the demon realm if eventually led to being with the mate he loved. "Yes. I would have done anything for my mate. You know that."

Athena nodded. "Your sister will eventually feel the same way. Give it time. It's over. Don't let your anger dampen your joy of seeing her again, and finding her alive."

"Did you know Sophie was in the demon realm?" Zach asked Athena suspiciously.

Even though Athena wasn't technically a goddess anymore because she'd become a *radiant* and then a mate to Hunter, the technicalities didn't mean shit. She still had the powers of a goddess, even after she'd given some of them to Hunter. And Zach knew damn well that she still got knowledge from the oracles at times.

Athena shook her head slowly. "No. I didn't know. I was given some garbled information, and I suspected Kristoff's mate was being held in the demon realm, but I wasn't certain. And I swear that I didn't know that his mate was your sister. I was as surprised as you were."

"I'm here now," Sophie said as she stood, and then moved to stand close to her brother. "The past doesn't matter. Like Athena said…it's over now." She hesitated before adding, "But I can never be Kristoff's mate."

"Why not?" Athena questioned sharply.

"I'm scarred, Athena, in case you haven't noticed," Sophie informed her in a self-deprecating tone. "A lot scarred. I barely remember human life, and I know very little about the Sentinels. The only information I got was through the Evils. Fate messed up. I knew I was a *radiant*, but I can't be Kristoff's."

Zach had been so damn happy to see Sophie's face that he'd barely thought about her scars, pox marks that had apparently never gone away. Looking at her now, he saw them, and he saw additional scars that had been inflicted during her time with the Evils. The scars affected him, but not in the way Sophie thought they did. His heart ached for every beating she'd suffered through; every mark they'd put on her body.

*Bastards!*

"Physical appearance doesn't matter to a Sentinel. You're not living in the human world anymore. It's different with a Sentinel mate," Athena explained. "He'll always want you. He'll always think you're the only perfect woman on the planet. Mating isn't about the superficial things. It's an elemental connection that will always draw you together."

"So it's not physical?" Sophie asked innocently.

Zach squirmed a little, not wanting to answer his sister's question. She'd never reached the age where he'd needed to discuss sex with her...thank God.

Luckily, Athena replied, "Oh, it's extremely physical, but the need to mate is in here." She pointed to her heart. "And here." She put a finger to her forehead.

*And then it travels to our dicks and we're totally screwed.* Zach didn't voice his thoughts, but he'd been through the experience of mating. It was like a chronic case of blue balls—times infinity.

Sophie was shaking her head. "How could he not notice how scarred I am? I scared some of the human women."

"I doubt it was you," Zach mumbled. "The shock of landing in the demon realm is enough to scare the hell out of anybody."

He still couldn't believe it—Sophie was Kristoff's *radiant*, and she was alive and well, even after centuries in the demon realm. He knew they'd used her, drained her of power as often as they could. Thinking about what she'd suffered at the hands of Goran made him nearly insane. As strong as she seemed, Sophie still needed healing. Lots of it. And most of her recovery wouldn't be physical. She was thin from lack of food, but she'd been taken to the demon realm as a child, and regardless of the pain that asshole Goran had caused Sophie, she was still in the dark about a lot of things. This world, *her* world, was foreign to her now.

"You can't kill Goran," Athena said matter-of-factly, as though she'd read Zach's mind. "I drained him of his excess power. Both Goran and Kristoff need to be alive in order for the balance to remain stable."

"How do you know?" Zach asked skeptically, hoping he could one day slay Goran for what he'd done to his sister.

Athena shrugged. "I might be a *radiant* now, but I still have many of my powers as a goddess. The oracles still speak to me."

Like he didn't know that? As sweet as Athena might appear, she was fierce, and she could kick the shit out of any of her Sentinels.

"How's Kristoff?" Drew asked as both he and Hunter got to their feet.

Athena's brows drew together thoughtfully. "Not as well as I had hoped. I've healed his physical injuries, but the toxins are bad, and he's still unconscious. Now that the poison has invaded his body, neither Talia nor I can help him. He's drawing into himself. I think he's having hallucinations and we can't seem to get him free."

Sophie let out an audible gasp. "He has to come back. Everybody needs him. I'll go up right now. Maybe he can hear me mentally."

Zach watched as his newfound sister sprinted up the stairs, still dressed in rags and looking like somebody had dragged her through Hell—which was, unfortunately, actually a pretty accurate description of what had been happening to her for the last few hundred years.

"I can't believe my sister is meant to be mated to Kristoff," he grumbled aloud.

"I thought you'd be happy," Athena commented, her brow raising expectantly as she looked at him.

"I'm happy and grateful to see my Sophie again. I thought she was dead a long time ago. But I'm not so sure I want *any* guy attached to her. Hell, she was just a kid when she disappeared. It's going to be rough thinking of her as an adult."

Zach knew what happened between mates, and just the thought of Kristoff messing with his sister that way made him wary. Granted, he was going to have to accept her as an adult woman, but it wasn't going to be easy.

Hunter commiserated, "You took care of her. You were her big brother. It is going to be hard to forget she's all grown up because you didn't see her becoming an adult."

"I agree," Drew added. "But Kristoff will take care of her. There's no one you'd trust with her more than him, and you know it."

Athena spoke in a quieter, thoughtful voice. "He is the right mate for her, Zach. I don't know any Sentinel who deserves a mate more than he does, even though he doesn't think so. He's waited a long time for this.

I think he gave up on ever finding his mate a long time ago. He doesn't think he deserves one, so he's going to be resistant to the idea himself."

Zach frowned, wondering why someone like Kristoff would feel unworthy, but he sensed that Athena wouldn't answer that question. "I know," he agreed. "I couldn't ask for anybody better. But I just found Sophie. I guess I want some time to make things up to her."

"It wasn't your fault," Athena answered. "If the Evils wanted her, they would have found another opportunity. It's obvious they knew she was special."

"Yeah, that's another thing. What's her gift, her unusual power? We have everything we need."

Athena shook her head. "That hasn't been revealed to me. I'm sorry. We won't know unless she mates with Kristoff."

"Is he going to make it?" Drew asked quietly, absently rotating Kristoff's ring on his finger uncomfortably, like he wanted it gone and back where it belonged.

"I should hope so," Athena replied. "If he was able to survive the torture of the Evils, he can certainly deal with the toxins. He has a lot more immunity to them than a regular Sentinel."

"I still feel like the balance is off," Drew remarked, sounding concerned.

"It will be off until Kristoff is well. With the amount of Evils we destroyed and after I drained Goran of his stolen power, we should be okay for a while. All we need is our king to be strong again. Just because the balance is restored, that doesn't mean that it always will be. The balance is a fragile thing, and we'll always have to be ready to deal with the Evils. Things will go on the same way they did before the gross imbalance started. Kristoff will need to recruit more Sentinels, and new *radiants* will be born. The Evils won't give up. They'll try harder than ever to gain power, and we'll still need to corral them. However, this time we'll be a lot more prepared."

"Will you lead us?" Zach asked curiously, wondering if the hierarchy would change now that their goddess creator was among them.

She shook her head emphatically. "No. Never. The power to lead has always been Kristoff's. He's critical to our survival now. If something happened to me, the world would go on. If something happens to him, we're all screwed. He has powers I don't possess; powers I gave to him that can never be given or taken back. Not to mention thousands of years of experience."

He nodded. Her explanation made sense. Athena had given Kristoff the power to create new Sentinels, broker deals, decide what designation each Sentinel would have, and he was a natural leader. Zach assumed Athena had created Kristoff, but his powers were something she didn't possess herself. Plus, when she designated him the king, it was something that could never be taken back, which was why it was so important for Kristoff to get well and take up his duties again. The originally appointed king was figured into the balance. Athena was not.

"Since he was taken against his will, I don't understand why he's feeling the toxins at all," Hunter questioned.

Athena shrugged. "The Evils have been ignoring the rules for a long time now. But you're right. I don't understand exactly why he seems so sick either. And it annoys me that I don't know the solution."

Zach wanted to laugh, but didn't. The goddess wasn't happy unless she had all the answers. Unfortunately, her powers didn't work that way. "He's not conscious at all?"

"He won't communicate, even to me. Although he's in an unconscious state, he should be able to talk to me telepathically now that he's back in the human realm. He either can't or won't. I'm not sure which."

"Those evil fuckers messed with his head," Hunter growled.

"Quite possibly," Athena conceded. "His injuries might be healed, but he's still weak from the torture, and for some reason he isn't able to wake up."

"What can we do?" Zach asked urgently, not wanting to see his sister crushed or Kristoff's demise. Although they looked around the same age, his king was like a father figure to him, and his mentor.

"Nothing right now. I'll let you know if there comes a time that we need you. Take your wives home and give them a rest. Sophie will be here, and I'll make sure she can reach any one of us if she needs to. You all fought well and hard. You all need rest."

Zach felt so edgy that he wasn't sure if he could even sleep. But he knew Kat had to be exhausted. She'd used everything she had today to get them into the demon realm. Athena was right. They all needed to sleep. But leaving his sister here wasn't going to feel right. She should be with him and Kat. Yeah, maybe she was Kristoff's *radiant*, but Zach still thought of Sophie as a child and probably would for a while.

On the other hand, Kristoff did need somebody to be with him while he was vulnerable.

"We can go see Kristoff and see if he'll listen to us, and then we'll take our women home," Hunter answered, giving Athena a warning look.

Athena held up a hand in defeat. "I'll go with you. If nothing else, I'll make you rest."

Zach watched as Hunter smiled at his goddess bride. He still couldn't believe that Hunter had finally found happiness. Hell, he still wasn't used to seeing Hunter smile.

His head turned toward the stairs that Sophie had raced up when she'd left, still stunned that she'd turned up alive after all these years.

*I have my sister back.*

It was difficult not to feel remorse over what she'd suffered, but he was going to enjoy the discovery of his only sibling being back where she belonged. Her life had been horrible, but he'd make it up to her. Eventually, her emotional scars would heal. And he had all the money in the world to take care of her. She'd want for nothing.

"I'll go, too," he told Hunter. "I want to say good-bye to Sophie and make sure she can contact me if anything changes. Then I can take Kat home. I think everybody is drained from fighting with the Evils."

All of them disappeared from the room to go look in on Kristoff, leaving the king's living room silent once more.

# Chapter Four

*K*ristoff felt his hand being lifted and someone, who he assumed was Drew, slipping his heavy ring back onto his finger. With the ancient symbol of the Sentinel king back in place again, it momentarily distracted him from the continual torture his mind was experiencing.

Having his symbolic ancient ring back on his finger felt right. It felt real.

But it didn't help much. Seconds later, he was plunged back into another nightmare, a place where he could easily forget everything, lapse into the experience as though it were real.

His hallucinations were mostly about his early years, but there were some that tormented him even more: the ones where his daughter was beheaded while he was rendered helpless. He had the same nightmares about Zach, Drew, and Hunter.

One right after the other.

There was no time to recover from the previous atrocity before he was experiencing the next.

*Kristoff? Come back to us. We need you.*

It was *her*, the woman who had saved him from insanity—or in his case, she'd tried to rescue him. He wasn't quite certain he *wasn't* crazy.

Her voice broke through the barrage of horror that was playing out in his mind for a moment, and he was able to reply.

*Can't come back right now. Too many Evil toxins.*

In his lucid moments, he knew what he was experiencing.

She answered.

*I thought you were immune. Athena didn't think it would affect you this much since you have some immunity and were there against your will.*

Her sweet but sultry voice wrapped around him, just like it had when they were in the demon realm together.

*Are you out, too?* He hoped to hell that she was.

*Yes.*

Relieved that she was no longer suffering and at the mercy of the demons, he explained why he was still expelling demon toxins.

*Athena failed to remember that I wasn't exactly there involuntarily. I struck a bargain and agreed to remain with the Evils in exchange for the release of Drew and Talia. I broke a vow.*

The woman paused, probably to explain to the other Sentinels if he was hearing correctly. The other voices were nothing but garbled sound, barely recognizable as belonging to his Sentinels. The only voice that was clear was *hers.*

Refusing to give in to the Evils' mind fuck, he fought back. He was back in the human realm. Trying to stay coherent, he reached out to the woman again.

*Talk to me. It helps.*

As long as the woman kept sending him mental messages and he fought hard for the connection between them, it kept the demon images at bay.

*What do you want to know?*

He didn't hesitate in responding.

*Is everyone safe? I could feel Drew returning my ring. But what about the others?*

She responded quickly.

*All of your friends are here. The Winstons and their mates are safe. What else do you want to know?*

He felt a weight lift from his chest just knowing that his daughter and friends had gotten through their crazy rescue plan.

*Tell me about you and why you were in the demon realm.*

Kristoff didn't much care what she said now that he knew that none of his friends had perished. He just wanted her to talk to him.

*My name is Sophie, and I'm actually Zach's sister. He thought I was dead, but I was in the demon realm all this time. Since I knew I was going to die anyway, I tried to bargain for his life. I didn't realize until much later that what I'd done was foolish. The Evils don't keep promises. You had already saved Zach, and I would have much rather died.*

What she was saying was almost unfathomable. Zach had sacrificed his humanity for Sophie, and she'd given her life to try to help her brother? Didn't the two of them realize how extraordinary they were, both of them so willing to give their life for their sibling? Zach had to be happy to see his sister, and it was a reunion Kristoff felt sad that he'd missed. He knew that although Zach was happy with Kat, there was a part of him that had never quite healed from Sophie's demise.

He'd had the feeling that one of the *radiants* being held was somehow connected to the Winstons, but he'd suspected the Evils might be harboring Hunter's mate. Obviously, his suspicion had been right about her being connected to the three brothers, but the reason was all wrong.

However, the fact that she hadn't died at the hands of Goran meant Sophie had to be a special *radiant*, one with an incredible dormant talent. For some reason, it bothered him that she was meant for another Sentinel.

She stopped talking, so he encouraged her. *What of the balance? Why is Athena here now? How did I manage to cheat death and escape from her hidden prison?*

Kristoff heard the background noise of other Sentinels talking in the background before her reply came.

*Athena is Hunter's radiant. He found her location and freed her from her imprisonment. Zach says she was the missing piece of the puzzle they needed to launch an attack. They're happy that the balance is almost equal again. Zach, Drew, Hunter and their radiants are fine. But they lost a few warrior Sentinels, and some will need much rest because of their injuries. Athena was able to revert Goran to his previous state, and take away the power he gained from sucking me and other women dry.*

*Fuck!* He'd been gone too long and had missed so much. It was very hard for him to believe that Hunter, of all people, was mated to a goddess. How in the hell had that happened? But Athena must have known or sensed something when she'd sent for his disturbed Sentinel. And he'd missed the entire battle, not to mention his own rescue. He took the death of *any* of his Sentinels hard, but he was grateful that his friends had made it through.

*So the balance is restored?*

Sophie was silent for a moment before she answered.

*Almost. We need you back, Kristoff. You and Goran still need to remain in your original states or things will continue to be slightly unbalanced.*

His body jerked involuntarily as he felt the butterfly touch of her fingers on his arm. It wasn't like he didn't *want* to wake up. He couldn't open his eyes. But the feel of Sophie touching him jolted at least part of him to life. He struggled to open his eyes, see the face connected to her sweet voice, but he knew that seeing her wouldn't be enough. He had to fucking feel her. Now!

*Kiss me!* He needed her warmth, her compassion, anything she'd give him right now. His previously cold body was suddenly heated to almost an excruciating heat.

Sophie was quiet, hesitating. *I'm not sure you'll be happy when you awake.*

*Why?*

Again, she was slow to answer. *I'm scarred from my smallpox, and scarred from my time in the demon realm. I'm not very attractive.*

He instantly hated the fact that she'd just belittled herself. *I don't care what you look like. I need you right now. Kiss me. Touch me, dammit!* He knew his tone was demanding, but if she didn't connect with him, he was going to lose his damn mind and spontaneously combust from the flames licking over his body.

*Christ!* It rankled for him to *need* anybody. But for some unknown reason, he *did* need Sophie. She'd kept him sane when he thought all hope for his mental state was gone. Because of her, he would eventually live in the human realm again, feel the sun on his face.

He breathed a sigh of relief as he felt her weight depress the mattress. He tensed, waiting for her to touch him.

Wanting...

Needing...

Angry because he couldn't reach out and take what he wanted himself.

Then, it happened. Her lips brushed against his lightly before she centered them and gave him a gentle kiss, one from lips so sweet that Kristoff felt his greedy demon rising inside him, wanting more.

*Not enough. It's not enough. More!*

Suddenly, he opened his eyes, wrapped a palm around her neck and deepened the kiss, devouring her mouth with a need so strong that the embrace went on and on.

The toxins were forgotten as Kristoff became consumed with something stronger than the demon mind fuck: the desire to own the woman he was holding, be the only one she'd ever need. All reason left him as he became obsessed with making her his, fucking her until she begged for mercy.

*Mine! Mine! Mine!*

Possessiveness like he'd never known flooded through his being as he speared his tongue into her mouth, and all he could think about was the animalistic urge to absorb this female into his very soul so no one could ever touch her again.

It made him crazy when he felt her answering need as her arms went around him, her tongue pushing back in an attempt to feel closer to him.

*Closer. More. More.*

He flipped her onto her back, trapping her beneath him, letting out a growl of satisfaction that she purred her approval and threaded her hands in his hair.

Both of them needed the same thing right now, their minds focused on one objective: for them to somehow merge. Kristoff was downright obsessed with the compulsion.

"Kristoff! For God's sake, let the poor girl go," Athena spoke as she stepped forward and removed Sophie from his grasp.

Closing his eyes because the pain of having Sophie so close, then separated from him was so damn painful, he let out a snarl of disapproval. He was panting from the deprivation of what he needed, what he wanted.

When he opened his eyes, the only thing he saw was his…*radiant*. Athena was standing next to her beside the bed, but Kristoff's eyes were riveted on nothing but Sophie.

His possessive instincts hit him hard even as he felt his soul grow slightly lighter as a small part of her soul drifted into his, and a minimal amount of darkness entered hers.

Covetous, greedy instincts slammed through him in that instant, and it was even worse than it had been a few minutes ago. Probably because he'd finally realized what Sophie was to him.

He grunted, the sound low and dangerous as it sprang from his throat. "Mine!"

Athena stepped forward and pushed him back onto his pillow. "She's an innocent, Kristoff, taken by Evils when she was a child. I know this is going to be difficult, but you can't just take what you want right now."

Oh yeah, he could. He needed to, and Sophie needed it, too. But he struggled to contain his demon instincts, concerned that he might alarm his mate. He was being driven by animal instincts, and he somehow needed to pull himself together.

His amber eyes slowly returned to a silvery blue as he stared at Athena angrily because she was blocking his vision of what belonged to him. "She's my *radiant*," he rasped, barely able to believe that he'd finally found his mate.

And Christ! It was as painful as it was surreal. Her light warmed him, but the need to make her his was nearly killing him.

*His* Sophie was beautiful, her long dark hair and chocolate-brown eyes mesmerizing him for the brief moment as their gazes met and held.

"He looks worse off than any of us ever were," Zach observed from his position closer to the door with the rest of the Winston crowd. "But I don't think I like seeing him manhandle my sister."

Kat elbowed Zach in the stomach. "You have no room to talk. As I recall, you "manhandled" me plenty. And it's obvious that Kristoff is hurting. When have we ever seen him like this? He doesn't have fits of anger, and he never loses control. He has to be in pain."

"He is," Athena informed them in a somber voice. "He's a demon king, the first of your kind. He's been without his mate for thousands of years. Take what you all felt and multiply it by a thousand."

"Shit!"

"Christ!"

"No way!"

Athena nodded her head. "That's what he's feeling right now."

The three Winston brothers were all shaking their heads and shooting Kristoff a sympathetic glance.

Zach stepped forward and put his arm around Sophie. "I won't tolerate him hurting my sister."

"She's Zach's sister?" both Talia and Kat asked in unison.

"She is," Drew affirmed. "Zach and I will catch you and Talia up on things later."

Athena turned and shot Zach an irritated look. "He'd die before he'd intentionally harm her. You know that."

"But unintentionally?" Zach pushed.

"I'm more afraid his intensity will frighten her," Athena admitted.

"I'm not afraid," Sophie said forcefully, pushing her way in front of Athena. "I *feel* him. For some reason we're sharing emotions. We're sharing thoughts. No matter what his reaction is, I don't think I could ever be afraid of him." She reached for Kristoff's hand, as though they both needed the connection.

Careful not to squeeze too hard, Kristoff clasped her small, delicate hand in his, feeling some of his anger slip away as she lit a part of his soul that had long been pitch dark. "You're as beautiful as your voice," he told her hoarsely, once again mesmerized by her gaze, and the determination he saw in her eyes.

She lowered her head. "I'm dirty, scarred, and I've been used by the demons for almost two centuries. That's not the mate for a king."

He missed seeing her eyes instantly, her hair cascading around her downturned face. "Don't ever look down in my presence," he demanded.

Her head popped up immediately. "I'm sorry."

"Don't be sorry, either," he insisted. "Athena, can you clean her up and dress her appropriately? My powers are weak right now. Her state of disarray obviously disturbs her."

With a wave of her hand, the goddess cleaned Sophie up and changed her into a pair of jeans and a soft, fuzzy, red, short sleeved sweater.

Kristoff's *radiant* ran a hand through her newly-repaired, silky dark hair, over the lightweight sweater, and finally brushed her fingers across the soft denim. "I've never worn pants before. I noticed the other women dressed like this. Times have changed?"

Athena snickered. "Honey, they've changed enormously. At least I had a TV to watch the changes. But you only have two hundred years to catch up with. I had eons. And you'll get used to wearing jeans. It took me a while."

"What is TV?" Sophie asked curiously.

Athena snatched the remote on Kristoff's bedside table and pushed a button. Sophie jumped as sound suddenly erupted from the television mounted on the wall.

As she handed Sophie the remote control, Athena proceeded to explained how to change the channels, and the difference between documentaries, reality TV, and fictional shows.

Kristoff's eyes never left his *radiant*, captivated by every little graceful motion she made, every word she said. The human realm was a strange new world for Sophie right now, but her curiosity would have her acclimating quickly.

*My mate. My radiant. Mine.*

His engorged cock throbbed with need, and the place where his mating mark should be burned like fire. He felt like he needed that mark more than he needed to breathe, and he was consumed with the desire to have his own on Sophie's shoulder.

"Zach and Drew need to take Kat and Talia home to rest," Athena told Kristoff.

"My *radiant* stays here with me," he demanded, unwilling to let Sophie leave his sight for even a moment. It had taken him thousands of years to find her. Honestly, he'd given up on ever being granted a mate. He sure as hell wasn't leaving anything to chance. He could already feel Sophie permeating his soul, her lightness chasing away the dark.

Then, his doubts started to plague him, the constant knowledge that had been with him since he became the Sentinel king.

*I don't fucking deserve a mate. She can't be mine. Even though I crave her, I'm going to have to set her free.*

The thought of Sophie *not* becoming his mate made a growl rise low in his throat. The desire to claim her was so strong that rational thought was difficult. His every instinct was to keep her close to him, bind her to him as quickly as possible.

But his humanity was speaking to him much more rationally, making him cautious and considering her feelings. It was his duty to make her happy, and she'd never be happy with him. Plus, she'd been a prisoner for two hundred years. All of her adult life. The last thing she needed was the burdens he carried heaped on her shoulders.

Sophie was everything that was light, curious, and compassionate, everything he'd never deserve because of his past.

"I'll stay with you," Sophie answered firmly.

Hearing her stand up to be with him made his soul brighter...and his cock harder.

"I'm putting you into a healing sleep for the night," Athena warned Kristoff. "I know you won't hurt Sophie intentionally, but as the Sentinel king who has finally found his mate, your emotions will be hard to control. You're not at your normal strength and your magic hasn't come back yet."

"No. I have to be able to protect her," Kristoff argued, knowing there was no fucking way he was sleeping and leaving his mate alone. Maybe he didn't deserve her, but right now, she was his to protect.

"The only danger she'll be in is from you," Athena answered sternly. "Guardian Sentinels are surrounding your palace right now. Be reasonable. You know your emotions are sitting on the edge of a very sharp blade right now. Until your magic returns completely, you'll lack the power to remain in control."

Kristoff wasn't feeling reasonable, and he didn't think the return of his magic was going to change a damn thing. He could sense it. Sophie was a temptation he wasn't going to control easily, even when he was operating at full strength.

Regrettably, Athena was right about one thing: his needs were raw and uncontrollable, but sleeping to recover his strength while his mate was trying to acclimate to the world in the twenty-first century wasn't sitting well with him. He wanted to be with her, and the demon part of him was selfish, covetous.

Except…it wasn't about his wants and needs right now. It was all about Sophie. He *wasn't* himself, and a night of induced sleep from a goddess would heal him faster than anything else would.

His need to be healthy and powerful to protect his mate was in-grained into his nature just as much as his need to bond with her was part of his soul. The two warring instincts were fighting with each other.

"Will we still be able to communicate?" Sophie asked curiously.

Athena nodded. "Yes."

"I'll stay right here with you, Kristoff. If you need me, just call out to me mentally." Sophie squeezed his hand.

Kristoff felt his more tender emotions temporarily take control because Sophie was so trusting, so innocent. Her faith in him and her willingness to stay beside him touched his soul.

"Do it before I change my mind," he instructed Athena gruffly. "I need my magic and my strength back. You and I both know that a half breed with my history doesn't deserve a mate, especially some-one like Sophie." He knew he was good for nothing except being the Sentinel king. It was his duty, and his salvation. He wouldn't tie Sophie to a Sentinel like himself. He couldn't. Somehow he had to fight the overpowering demands of his soul and his body.

He gritted his teeth and squeezed Sophie's hand, satisfied that she'd be safely beside him through the night with guardians around his mansion. Maybe he couldn't bond her to him for life, but for now, she was his to protect.

"You're wrong, Kristoff. Nobody deserves a *radiant* more than you." Athena lifted her hand, and Kristoff's eyes drifted closed, his brain shutting down as he fell into a dreamless sleep.

Not very long after he slept, his mind sensed Sophie moving onto the bed next to him and settling in beside him, her emotional and physical warmth giving him peace.

For now, it was enough to know she was here, right beside him.

He slept, feeling a sense of contentment that he'd never experienced during a very long existence. His body might still burn to possess her, and his soul was clamoring to be merged with hers. But he focused on the temporary light she brought to his soul, and the miracle of *her*.

Kristoff had a living, breathing *radiant*, a woman who just happened to be Zach's long lost sister. Zach had suffered without Sophie, but Kristoff knew he'd go through hell himself if he could manage to somehow separate the bond between them.

As he rested, Kristoff vowed that he'd make Sophie happy, help her catch up on all she'd missed—before he had to let her go.

His body tensed, but he pushed his complicated issues aside as he gave into sleep. Maybe he couldn't keep Sophie, but she was here *now*, and that would have to be enough.

# Chapter Five

*I*t was late before Sophie finally climbed quietly off the bed where Kristoff rested and went to the closet of clothing Athena had manifested before she and the rest of the Winstons had finally left Kristoff's residence. Absently, she searched for what looked like sleeping attire, and finally pulled a nightgown from the closet and pulled it on after removing all of the clothing that the goddess had used to dress her.

She'd spent a lot of time watching television, trying to catch up on everything she had missed. Some of what she saw was almost unbelievable. Women wore pants often, and skirts that barely covered their behind.

It seemed that women didn't *need* a man in the twenty-first century, but many still chose to marry. Men could marry other men, and a woman could marry another woman, something that wasn't even whispered about when she'd been a child.

*So much has changed.*

Sophie felt like a fish out of water, still not able to comprehend how different the world was today compared to how it had been two hundred years ago. Women's roles had definitely evolved, and they could actually vote, hold important political offices, or be professionals.

Wandering into the bathroom suite, she marveled at the plumbing, sighing as she saw the bath tub, knowing now that she could turn the knobs and it would fill with hot water.

*Everything is so much easier.*

The human realm was filled with wonders and luxuries that she could have never imagined as a child. She and Zach had lived in poverty during their childhood, but even if they hadn't, none of these things had existed in their time. The rich had just had far more servants to keep from being inconvenienced with the trivial tasks.

Pulling at the hem of the nightwear, which felt strange to her because it didn't touch the floor, Sophie went to the bed and crawled between a set of sheets that were so luxurious that she wasn't sure she'd ever want to get out of bed.

She'd never really had a bed to sleep in, and it felt decadent and wonderful.

Lying next to her, his broad chest rising and falling rhythmically, was Kristoff, his chest bare, and the sheets down around his waist. The sleep that Athena had put him into must be working well, because he hadn't moved. He hadn't reached out to communicate with her either, even though Athena had said it would be possible.

Tentatively, she put a palm against his chest, marveling at the smooth skin that covered so much muscle. She stroked his hard shoulders and chest before moving downward to trace his well-defined six pack abs with her index finger. Curiously, she followed the line of fine, blond hair that trailed from below his belly button and disappeared underneath the sheet.

"You're so handsome," she spoke aloud, turning her attention to his face. In sleep, he looked like he was at peace with the world. His beautiful mane of light blond hair was just long enough to make her itch to run her fingers through it. "Why was I, of all people, chosen to be your *radiant*?"

*He thinks I'm beautiful. He didn't even seem to notice my scars. How crazy is that?*

Just like Athena had claimed, Kristoff couldn't seem to see any of her imperfections. He looked at her like he wanted to devour her whole, and Sophie couldn't stop remembering how the same emotions had surged up inside her when he'd kissed her: the need, the longing, the desperation to have Kristoff claim her. In his unguarded moments, their embrace had been feral and all-consuming.

*I have to stop thinking about how I felt when he touched me. He himself told Athena he didn't want to bond with me.*

The thought consumed her with an overwhelming sadness.

She was all wrong for this fierce male, the King of the Sentinels. With her scarred face and her past—including her human life as a street urchin—Sophie knew she'd never be this man's mate. He was too gorgeous, too royal, too wise, too powerful…too much of everything.

*Feeling a man up when he's helpless is cruel, Sophie. It could get you into a lot of trouble when I finally wake up.*

She startled at the rumble of Kristoff's voice in her head, mortified that she had been fondling him when he was unable to rebuff her. Really, it *was* pretty rude to be fondling him as he slept. But it was hard for her to control her actions when he was lying right next to her. Even if she could never be his, the instincts of her soul and body were clamoring for their mate.

She backed off to her side of the massive bed.

*I'm sorry. That was inappropriate.* She was instantly contrite. Touching him had been so wrong for so many reasons, not to mention making her ache for him more than she had before she'd touched him again.

*Never be sorry for touching me. As your mate, I'd always welcome it. It's the way of Sentinel mates. But right now, all I can think about when I feel your hands on me is claiming you.*

He'd seen her quite clearly. Why would he *want* to touch her?

He answered as he picked up her thoughts. *Because to me, you're the most beautiful woman I've ever seen. Do you have any idea how long I've waited for my radiant? How many times I was certain my mate had somehow perished.*

She shook her head, even though he couldn't see her. *No. But I'm not fit to be the mate of the Sentinel king. You know what Zach and I were as children. And I've been used and defiled by demons for two hundred years, Kristoff. I've been gone so long I don't know how to function in this world. This is all some kind of mistake.*

*It's not a mistake. You. Are. Mine.*

Sophie shivered at the primitive tone in his communication, but it wasn't fear that caused the reaction. Her body began to go up in flames, and she desperately needed…something. Her core clenched, and she felt a flood of heat rush between her thighs.

Whatever Kristoff was feeling, she felt it, too, and it was a connection so elemental that she ached to be part of him, even though she barely knew him.

*Don't over think this, Sophie. The mating connection is strong, almost powerful enough to overcome Athena's magic. Sleep. It's been a long day for you, and I can sense your weariness. Come back to me. I feel better when you're close.*

She frowned as she answered. *I thought it was painful.*

He answered with strained amusement. *I'm screwed either way because it hurts when you aren't touching me, too.*

Sophie moved back to Kristoff's side of the bed. *I'm starting to think that having a radiant is more of a curse than a blessing.*

His powerful voice came back to her quickly. *No! A radiant is never a curse. You put light in my soul, and you take away the emptiness. Being bonded mates is intimate and special. It's the one good thing that happens for Sentinels. It's just the mating heat that really sucks.*

Sophie reached out instinctively and touched his bare shoulder. *I burn here. And I feel like my body is about to catch on fire. Is that the mating heat?*

He let out a mental groan before answering. *Yeah. That's where the mating mark appears. And the heat is from the need to be joined together.*

Even as Kristoff spoke telepathically, Sophie was yawning. She snuggled up close to him and put her head on his chest, comforted when she heard the strong beat of his heart. Trust shouldn't come easy to her, but for some reason, she felt safer being next to him. *Goodnight, Kristoff.*

He made a mental noise that sounded like something between a growl and purr, a sound of complete satisfaction before she closed her eyes and fell instantly into a peaceful slumber.

"She has to accept that she's his *radiant* and bind herself to him," Athena said the next morning as she paced the kitchen in the colorfully decorated home she shared with Hunter. "I'm not sure he'll ever be right unless she does. He had to wait too long, and his hunger is going to be powerful. I'm not sure he'll stay sane if he doesn't."

Hunter looked up from the table where he was tearing into his breakfast. "You have doubts that she will?"

"She has to do it soon. But she hesitates. I can feel her reluctance. And even though finally finding his *radiant* is almost a miracle, Kristoff is reluctant, too. I think she's as attracted to him as he is to her. But she doesn't feel like she's his true *radiant*. And my stubborn king is never going to convince himself that he deserves her because of his own past. They are both going to be pigheaded when they actually have so much in common. They'd understand each other if they just try."

"She'll figure it out as soon as he gets her naked. There's no way he's going to be able to hold out for long," Hunter replied with a smirk.

Athena gave her husband an irritated glare. She loved Hunter with everything she had, but he was still a smartass at times. "He needs time to understand he won't survive without her. It's mating dance time, and they both need to get in step."

Hunter shrugged. "Then they can dance naked."

"This isn't a joke," Athena snapped. "I don't want to lose Kristoff. You know what he is to me, and he was loyal to me before the demons were even created."

As though he sensed the distress in his *radiant's* tone, Hunter got up and stood in front of her, causing her to slam into his body as she turned to pace a different direction.

The goddess sighed as their bodies collided, loving Hunter's powerful form against hers. She could never stay mad at him, which irritated the hell out of her. He took her wrists and put her arms around his neck. "Kiss me," he demanded.

"Hunter, this is no time to—"

He pulled her head back with her long braid and covered her mouth with his. As always, Athena caved in, opening to him so he could have what they both wanted. For a brief moment, her troubles faded and all she could feel was Hunter.

As he finally released her mouth, she murmured, "Why do you always do that?"

"Because it's the only way I can get you to calm down. Besides, you're sexy when you're all worked up." He paused, taking her face between his palms as he added, "Stop worrying. Kristoff knows what he's doing. I've always had faith in him as a king, even though I was a jackass at times."

"Maybe he's wise in all other things except this. But he's never experienced the mating urge, and nobody is ever going to experience it the way he does."

"He'll be fine," Hunter grumbled, kissing Athena's forehead.

"He'll be stubborn. He dedicated himself to spending the rest of his existence keeping the Evils in check and watching over my Sentinels. Honestly, I think he has always been hoping he'd never find his *radiant*, even though he secretly yearns for one, as all Sentinels do. I don't want to lose him. I've been terrified for him since I found out he'd been taken by the Evils. If Sophie hadn't been there, I'm not sure he would have ever been the same. He has a chance at a normal life now, a happy life. But I know Kristoff. He'll sacrifice himself before he does something he thinks will hurt somebody else."

"We aren't going to lose him," Hunter rumbled.

"Are we ready to go wake up Sleeping Beauty?" Drew asked as he popped into the room with Talia at his side.

Athena turned, feeling more reassured as Hunter grasped her hand and threaded his fingers through hers. "I suppose we should."

Athena knew she was going to have to send Kristoff and Sophie away, someplace that would calm her Sentinel king. And she knew exactly where they needed to go.

"We'll go, too," Zach chimed in as he appeared next to Drew with Kat by his side. "We've been trying to wait until a decent hour, but I want to see my sister. Leaving her alone last night didn't feel right to me."

Athena nodded. "I understand. But Kristoff needs her more right now. You'll have eternity to spend with your sister."

The goddess knew Zach wanted to be with his sibling. Losing Sophie had nearly destroyed Zach, but he'd have to delay a full reunion until his king was stable and safely mated.

Zach frowned. "Is Sophie really Kristoff's mate? It just seems so surreal that she's actually a *radiant*, that she's really alive. I've spent so many years trying to accept her death. Now that she's alive, it doesn't seem possible that she's not gone, that she was *never* really gone."

"She's definitely his *radiant*," Athena answered emphatically. "Couldn't you feel the power in the room last night?"

"I think all of us felt it," Zach acknowledged. "It won't be easy to let her go. I still think of Sophie as a child, as my responsibility."

"Tread lightly," Athena warned. "If Kristoff senses your possessiveness, even in a brotherly way, he's likely to lose it. Have patience, Zach. You've waited two hundred years to see your sister again. Kristoff has waited thousands of years for his mate, even though he doesn't realize it yet."

"I'd like to see them together," Drew commented quietly. "Kristoff deserves to be happy, and Sophie couldn't have a better or more loyal mate."

"Kristoff deserves peace more than you know," Athena muttered under her breath. Her demon king hadn't seen much real joy in his very long life. He was entitled to every bit of sweetness he could get from Sophie.

Not hearing Athena's comment, Drew continued, "If Sophie was his true mate, how did he sire a daughter with another woman?"

Talia broke into the conversation. "It was fated. It's in the prophecies. He was meant to be my father, and I was born to be a special *radiant*. The explanation was a little vague, but I needed a powerful father to develop my talent to restore power in the demon realm."

All three Sentinels rolled their eyes as Drew spoke. "The prophecies? You mean you still believe in those?"

"Yes."

"Yes."

"Yes."

Athena, Talia and Kat spoke in unison, and then burst into laughter.

"Why wouldn't we," Talia answered. "Every one of them has come true. Maybe some of it only made sense after it occurred, but the prophecies are very, very real."

"Coincidence," Hunter muttered. "The words are so vague that they could be interpreted a thousand different ways."

"Say what you want, but we know they were accurate," Talia answered irritably. "I'd like to spend time getting to know my father after all this is over."

Athena heard the longing in Talia's tone. "You will," she assured her friend. "Just let's get them mated before your dad loses his mind."

"What do we need to do?" Kat asked curiously.

"Somehow, we need to convince Sophie that she really is Kristoff's mate. Neither one of them feel worthy of the other, and it's going to cause problems. I think we need to take her aside and explain, make her realize that what she's feeling, Kristoff is experiencing a thousand times stronger. Because of her past, her scars, and her years in the demon realm, she doesn't feel like she's Kristoff's match. We need to get her past that. Make her realize exactly how the Sentinel mating bond works."

"She doesn't understand that Kristoff will always see her as beautiful and perfect?" Kat asked curiously. "Of course, I found that hard to believe at first, too."

"You are perfect," Zach said adamantly.

"But I didn't feel beautiful back then. I felt like a fat, ugly woman who no decent man would ever want. I understand what it's like to feel unwanted and broken. Sophie has been used and hurt for centuries, Zach. Her self-esteem has to be in the toilet by now."

Seeing the dangerous look on Zach's face, one that said he wanted to take Kat right there up against the wall to prove how much he wanted her, Athena said quickly, "We'll figure out a way to explain things to her. Are we ready to go?"

All three men nodded, and one by one, the couples disappeared.

# Chapter Six

Sophie was relieved when Athena appeared abruptly in Kristoff's bedroom with Hunter at her side.

Normally, it might be frightening to have people popping in and out of rooms in the human realm, but Kristoff had become so agitated that she was relieved to see the Winstons arrive one-by-one.

She jumped off the bed and raced to throw herself in her brother's arms as he appeared, marveling at just how handsome he'd become. He'd been a young man, little more than a child himself, the last time she'd seen him. Now, he was all grown up, a different man, yet somehow she could still see the boy she knew in his eyes.

"Zach!" she exclaimed as she hugged him enthusiastically. It didn't feel the least bit awkward anymore. He was still her brother, and Sophie was starting to remember more and more of their past.

Her elder brother had always put her first, taken on the responsibility of caring for his sister without a single complaint. She had always gotten any food he'd managed to either steal or beg for on a street corner. Zach would have died of malnutrition to keep *her* alive, but she'd forced him to eat by threatening to not eat unless he did.

When she'd contracted smallpox, he'd sacrificed everything to be at her side in one of the hovels where they put the sick and dying.

*I'll make it better for us, Sophie. Please, just don't leave me here alone.*

It was one of the last things she remembered Zach saying to her before he'd left, promising to return with food, water, and better accommodations for both of them.

She hadn't been able to fulfill his request. Sophie *had* left him alone.

She'd never seen him again until yesterday, the brother who had cared so much for her and been cruelly wiped from her memories by the Evils. She'd remembered how much she'd grieved for her brother, making trouble for the demons when she'd looked for every avenue of escape. Then one day, she just couldn't remember much anymore. They'd stolen Zach from her, and she was just grateful to get those memories back.

Tears trickled down her face as she held onto him tightly, relieved that she was now remembering her years with Zach. Somehow, the Evils had taken her memories, but she was slowly taking back what was stolen from her in the demon realm. "You were such a good brother," she said as she sniffled and pulled back to look at her brother's face. "And you grew up so handsome and strong."

He'd been stick thin as a child. They both had been. But unlike her, Zach had filled out and turned into a very handsome Sentinel.

"You remember more?" Zach asked hesitantly.

"Pretty much everything. It came back slowly, but I remember our struggles together as children. I remember how much you tried to take care of me, even though you were just a boy yourself. You only ever asked one thing from me, and I couldn't do it. I'm sorry I left you," she said remorsefully.

He took her by the shoulders. "It wasn't your fault, Soph."

Her heart lifted as Zach used the nickname he'd used for her as a child. "I know. But it's ironic that I thought I was going to save you, and you thought the same thing when you pledged your life to the Sentinels to save me."

Her brother frowned as he grumbled, "My deal was a hell of a lot better than yours. Kristoff took me into his home and mentored me, and I had everything I'd ever dreamed of having as a kid. Everything except my sister."

"But he wasn't happy," Kat said as she broke into the conversation. "Materially, he had everything he wanted. But he never forgave himself for leaving you to die alone."

Sophie's gaze focused on her brother. "Is that true?"

He nodded slowly. "I shouldn't have left you. Or I should have made another wish, one that would have saved you back then. Foolishly, I thought money would solve all of our problems."

Sophie placed her hand on his forearm, her heart hurting because of the guilt Zach had carried for so long. "It wasn't your fault. Nothing that happened to us was our fault, but you tried so hard to keep me safe. I could blame myself because you gave your human self to the Sentinels for me."

"I don't regret it. If I didn't, I wouldn't have met Kat. And I wouldn't have been there to save her. And I wouldn't be here for you now."

"Then let it go, Zach," Sophie pleaded. "The memories of the demon realm will eventually fade. I'm here now. I have to believe all of this was somehow fated."

"It was," Talia affirmed as she and Drew came to stand beside them. "You were meant for Kristoff, his destined mate. It's all in the demon prophecies."

Sophie saw her brother and Drew roll their eyes as the latter remarked, "She was fated to suffer in the demon realm for over two hundred years? It says that in the prophecies?"

"Not exactly," Talia admitted. "But it does mention that the king's mate will be challenged and found worthy only after suffering true torment."

"Two hundred years in the demon realm is more than just torment. It's fucking inhumane," Zach rumbled.

Sophie looked from Talia to her brother. "You and Drew don't believe in the prophecies?" she questioned.

"No."

"No."

They both answered in unison.

Talia took her by the hand and pulled Sophie to her side. "Don't listen to them. Let me tell you about the demon prophecies. Every one of them matches up with what really happened."

Sophie listened intently as Talia explained what had been foretold. Athena and Kat joined them and verified that the ancient demon scrolls were accurate.

"Did it say anything else about Kristoff?" she asked breathlessly, wondering if they knew his fate.

"No," Talia answered sadly. "All they say at the end is that his fate will be decided by the one who is worthy if she survives her test." She paused before adding, "That's you. His *radiant*. As a scholar and a person who has studied the prophecies, I think that means his fate is in your hands. You can either accept him or destroy him. You've earned that right by surviving in the demon realm."

"How is it possible for a woman to have that kind of power over a king?" Sophie asked nervously, not comfortable with deciding *anyone's* destiny. "And how is it possible that a child of the streets and an escapee from the demon realm is meant to be Kristoff's mate? I'm nobody special."

"Kristoff wasn't always a king," Athena answered quietly. "I bestowed him with that title when he became my first Sentinel. And Talia is right. If you don't accept him as your mate, he'll cease to exist as he did before. He is meant to have a strong partner, a queen to stand at his side. He's lived in total darkness without the light of a *radiant* for too long. To finally find you and then not be mated to you would destroy him."

"So I have no choice but to be his mate?" Sophie asked hesitantly.

"You have a choice," Athena told her. "But Kristoff is going to be a very hard Sentinel to ignore, and he'll do everything in his power to fight the mating. He has his own doubts about whether or not he deserves a *radiant*, but he needs you more than he's ever needed anything or anyone in his entire existence."

Sophie's heart skittered. Nobody had ever needed *her*, and she couldn't imagine the gorgeous man lying in bed just a few feet away would actually want *her*.

*I do want you. I just can't take you as my mate. You've suffered enough.*

Sophie startled as Kristoff's gruff voice sounded in her head.

"You okay, Soph?" Zach asked in a concerned tone.

She'd been staring into space, listening to Kristoff's comment. "I'm fine," she answered distractedly. "Why is he so reluctant if he knows I'm his destined mate?" She directed her question to Athena.

Athena answered carefully. "He has his own secrets, and they aren't mine to tell. But believe me when I say that he doesn't believe he deserves anything good."

"When do I need to decide?"

The goddess smiled. "As long as you can hold out against his attempts to seduce you. Eventually his nature will overcome his resistance."

The women spirited her away to the corner of the room, and Sophie continued to ask questions about the mating process and exactly how it worked. Kat, Athena and Talia shared some of their own experiences, and generally filled Sophie with as much information as she could absorb at one time.

Finally, Sophie glanced at the bed and stared at the muscular form and gorgeous face of the man who was still under the sleep induced by the goddess. He was perfect. Kristoff was a king, a male made up of strength and power. Even though she understood how the mating of Sentinels worked, she still had a hard time believing she was his chosen *radiant*.

*Believe it. My darkness is already lighter. I may even forgive Athena if she gets me out of this damn sleep spell now.*

Sophie smiled as she turned to Athena. "He wants to wake up, and he's getting cranky."

The goddess rose her arm gracefully, murmuring a few words in what sounded like an ancient language Sophie didn't understand.

Kristoff didn't wake slowly. He bolted upright on the bed, his light blue eyes growing darker instantly as his gaze focused unwaveringly on her.

His stare turned a brilliant amber, and Sophie turned her head without thought, trying to hide her face.

"Never try to hide from me," Kristoff growled as he appeared at her side. "Never try to shield yourself away from anyone. You're beautiful, and your scars are part of your character. You're brave and strong. Never shy away from who you are."

She turned in surprise, marveling at the powerful glow of his eyes, a light so strong it cast an amber tint to the entire room.

Sophie knew the color of his eyes was a direct result of his desire for his mate. "I'm a disappointing mate, don't you think?" Meeting his stare, she tilted her chin so he could see her, scars and all.

He was right. Being fearful was no way to begin her relationship with him. If he rejected her physical appearance, so be it. But his words and his character gave her a courage like she'd never known. She had no need to hide from anyone. She might not always be comfortable in her own skin, but her scars were part of her past, part of her. People were either going to accept or reject her for something that was beyond her control. Honestly, those who judged her by her appearance weren't the kind of friends she wanted anyway.

He reached for her chin and tilted her head up even farther. "Never say you aren't beautiful. I feel your light, I share your mind, and I know your soul."

Strangely enough, she believed him because she was starting to know him, too. She sensed his darkness, felt the pain of the centuries of isolation he'd endured. To be a king required a certain aloneness and separation. "You've been alone for a long time," she murmured, the words leaving her lips uncensored.

He nodded abruptly, knowing immediately what she meant by her observation. "I always have been."

"But you weren't always a Sentinel," she said, cocking her head as she observed his fierce expression.

"Time for us to depart, I think," Athena said abruptly.

Kristoff looked at Athena, then his eyes drifted over the Winstons. "Everyone disobeyed me except for Athena. What do you have to say for yourselves? It was foolish to risk your lives just to save me. I'll have an explanation before you go."

"It wasn't just for you, although we would have risked everything to get you out of there. You know that. The balance was tilted too far. The Evils would have overrun the human realm," Drew answered.

"What happened?" Kristoff questioned abruptly.

Hunter, Zach and Drew quickly caught him up on all that had occurred while Kristoff had been a prisoner of Goran's, and how Athena had come to be free and a *radiant* to Hunter. They went on to explain that Hunter and Athena had given them what they needed to shift the balance back into place.

Kristoff moved forward and slapped Hunter on the back. "So you can finally live a normal life."

Hunter grinned at his king without malice. "I don't know how normal it is to be a Sentinel with a goddess as my mate, but yeah, I'm pretty damn happy."

"I wish I had known that your loss of control wasn't your fault, that you were destined to help normalize the balance as an equalizer."

"Don't be sorry," Hunter requested huskily. "I'd do it all again to end up where I am right now—with Athena. If my actions helped her survive, I'd gladly take the punishment as many times as necessary."

"You're happy?" Kristoff asked Athena bluntly.

"Very happy," she answered honestly.

Sophie saw the goddess's look of adoration as she watched and listened to Hunter. It was obvious that Athena felt the same way as Hunter did. What would it be like to love a man that much, to be so completely bonded to him?

"I suppose I missed the wedding?" Kristoff asked gruffly.

Hunter shrugged. "It was short and done at the courthouse after our men could establish a human identity for Athena. You didn't miss a big celebration. We were too damn busy trying to save the world."

Kristoff nodded, as though he understood that there had been no time for anything but trying to keep the human realm safe.

"It's going to be difficult to do damage control in this realm. The Evils have exposed themselves to so damn many humans," Kristoff observed solemnly. "Don't get too comfortable. The Evils will always be a threat, and restoring the balance doesn't lessen our responsibilities in the future."

Drew spoke up, "We're working on it. Everything has calmed down some. There are still some memories that need to be erased, and we have Evils to slay in this dimension. We'll get it under control again. But all of us know our job will be never-ending. But I have to admit that it will be nice to get back to business as usual instead of operating with looming world destruction in play."

"I'm going to need some time with Sophie to figure out our... situation," Kristoff rumbled. "I'll leave you all in charge of damage control. We need to get life back to normal as quickly as possible, and become an unknown fighting force to humans again."

Sophie wasn't exactly happy with being Kristoff's "situation." He hadn't said whether it was good or bad, but he certainly didn't sound overjoyed about spending time with her.

Honestly, she wasn't quite sure how she felt about being his *radiant* either, so maybe they did need time to work things out.

"I'm helping," Athena added. "I still have most of my goddess powers, so I can reverse the mistakes here quickly. We'll right things here, Kristoff."

"How are my men?"

Zach replied, "The ones that were injured are healing. We haven't lost any more."

"Good to hear," Kristoff answered, sounding relieved. "Do your best to continue on until I return."

"Where are you going?" Zach asked, sounding concerned.

"Your sister needs to see and experience the changes that have taken place while she was in the demon realm. We can't ignore the fact that we're mates. It has to be dealt with," Kristoff explained.

"I don't like you leaving with her," Zach said plainly.

"I know," the king replied solemnly as he took Sophie's hand.

Her heart pounded with anticipation. "Where are we going?"

While she appreciated her brother's concern, her heart ached to go away with the formidable Sentinel king. Not only did she want to see the progress the world had made since she'd been taken away, but she was yearning to spend time with her supposed match. Kristoff mesmerized her, tempted her toward things she'd never known.

Judging by the way her body responded to nothing more than a simple touch from Kristoff, and considering Athena's warning about Kristoff's mental state, it was clear they did need to resolve the mate thing as quickly as possible.

*What is the world like now? I've seen things on TV, but was it fiction or reality?*

For so long, she'd seen only darkness. She was more than ready to walk into the light of the human realm again.

"Any place you want to go," Kristoff answered in a deep voice that beckoned her to imagine the places he could take her.

He held out his hand.

Completely on instinct, Sophie didn't hesitate to place her smaller palm in his, and let him lead her wherever he wanted to go. "Show me." It was a statement with a little bit of a question included.

He nodded once, his eyes changing to an ocean-blue hue as he turned to Zach. "I'll bring her back safely. You'll have to trust me. Don't do it because I'm your king. Have faith in me because I've always been your friend and your mentor. I'd die before I'd see your sister come to any harm."

Kat took Zach's hand as he stared at Kristoff, silently supporting her mate.

Finally, Sophie's brother nodded. "You raised me, taught me what I needed to know. You saved me. I'm not sure where I'd be right now if I'd lost Sophie and we'd never met. Obviously, I'd be long dead by now, and I doubt I would have lived long after Sophie was taken away." He paused before adding, "But this isn't easy for me. You have to remember that Sophie didn't have a good childhood, and then was imprisoned in the demon realm for two centuries. She deserves happiness now. She's my sister and I love her."

Sophie's eyes filled with tears as Zach so easily said the words she'd wanted to hear for so long. "I love you, Zach. And I'll be back. This is something I need to do."

Zach nodded. "I understand."

"We all have catching up to do," Kristoff rumbled, keeping Sophie close to his side. "I have a daughter I very much want to know better."

Talia smiled at her father. "I want that, too. Very much."

Sophie could see the longing in Talia's eyes as she looked at Kristoff. She'd gathered that Talia was Kristoff's daughter, but she hadn't known the whole story until the women had pulled her aside earlier. Now, she understood that Talia wanted to know Kristoff as a father, just as she wanted to get to know who her brother was now.

"I know a good place for you two to deal with this situation," Athena said thoughtfully, then lifted her hand to send the two of them on their way.

Kristoff and Sophie disappeared instantly.

"Where did you send them?" Hunter asked curiously.

"Paradise. A place where they can find each other," she answered with a smile. "Now let's get moving and clean up the mess the Evils made so we can live a normal life again. Maybe once our work is done, we can all take the honeymoons we never had because we were too busy trying to save the world."

"Somewhere warm and tropical," Kat added with a look of longing on her face.

"On a beach where I can lay around naked all day if I don't feel like getting dressed," Talia agreed with a nod.

Drew's brow lifted in surprise as he looked at his mate, but he was the first one to disappear with Talia, obviously anxious to be gone if it meant he was going to have plenty of naked time with his wife when they could get things done.

Hunter and Zach left with their *radiants* moments later, obviously motivated by the same thoughts.

# Chapter Seven

"Where are we?" Sophie asked, looking around frantically as they flashed into the destination where Athena had sent them with her magic.

Kristoff clenched his fists as he watched Sophie twirl around, trying to look at everything at once. He knew exactly where they were. Even before they'd appeared at Athena's secret hideaway, he'd known where she'd send him the moment she'd used her powers as a goddess to send them someplace secure and private.

*The only place I've ever been happy. The only safe place I ever knew.*

"Athena's old private residence," he told Sophie, unable to tear his eyes away from her astonished expression. "Almost no one even knew it existed, especially none of the gods."

His eyes devoured her; his body craved her.

*Mine!*

His soul burned, and his cock was hard enough to chop wood.

How much longer could he be her tour guide and make polite conversation before he nailed her to the wall and fucked her so hard that she didn't know where her body ended and his began. He needed to make her come so hard that she couldn't remember her own name, and never wanted another man again.

The breeze carried her scent, and his nostrils flared as he smelled some of the same desires he was feeling floating into his lungs every time he took a labored breath.

*Fuck!*

Sophie was the ultimate temptation to him, but he was determined not to give in. His healing sleep had restored his power. Still, not letting his demon instincts gain control was nearly impossible. Nothing about his mate inspired control. She made him feel more alive than he ever had in his entire existence, and the desire to claim what was his was overpowering. Not acting on those emotions was painful as hell.

He wanted another taste of her beautiful mouth. He wanted his cock buried inside her until she screamed his name and was vowing to be his for eternity.

"Are we still in the human realm?" she queried.

Kristoff shook his head slowly, his body shuddering with the effort of not reaching out for her. "No. This was once Athena's secret residence, a place she created for solitude. We're in the land of the gods. But this space belonged entirely to Athena. This was the only place she could be alone. The only place she could be herself when she was a goddess."

"You've been here before," Sophie stated as she raised her foot and then scrunched her toes in the pristine white sand on the beach.

Kristoff had dressed himself in jeans and a blue button down shirt as they'd traveled. But he was shoeless just like Sophie, and he relished the sound of the pounding waves on the beach as his feet sank comfortably into the calming grains of sand. Sophie was wearing the same outfit Athena had given her after cleaning her up yesterday. She must have changed earlier that morning because he distinctly remembered feeling her body against his, nothing but the light cotton of her nightgown between them, and he'd relished the warm softness of her body against him. It had been sweet fucking torture. He grimaced as his wayward dick throbbed painfully; every moment he watched Sophie was both bliss and agony.

Tearing his eyes away from her with considerable effort, he quickly noted that Athena's paradise looked exactly as she'd left it. The water was still a mesmerizing shade of blue, and her castle still intact.

"I lived here for a time," Kristoff admitted reluctantly, not really wanting to talk about his life as a demigod.

"With Athena?" Sophie asked as she looked at him curiously.

"Yes," he answered simply. Able to share Sophie's thoughts, he added, "We were never lovers. Athena was my mentor." He both loved and hated the fact that he could sense Sophie's momentary jealousy. His mate wasn't the type to be envious, but her *radiant* instincts brought out a covetous nature that was natural for Sentinel mates. Right now, that possessive instinct coming from Sophie was like an aphrodisiac. As much as he wanted to claim her, he wanted her to recognize him as hers, too. Her covetous emotions fanned the flames that he didn't think could get any hotter.

He felt greediness, too, and on a much stronger level than Sophie did. Every cell in his body was clamoring for him to claim his mate, brand her as his, and make sure she stayed by his side forever. The longing pierced him in the gut like a sharp knife that was twisting into him over and over.

"I can't imagine what it would be like to live here."

Kristoff shrugged. "It was Athena's version of paradise."

"I think it's mine, too," Sophie answered breathlessly. "It's beautiful here."

He had to clench his fists to stop from reaching out and capturing his *radiant* so he could feel her slight body against his.

*Christ! I've fought for my life against both gods and demons, but one tiny, beguiling female has me tied up in knots!*

His emotions were conflicted. Although he was stunned that he'd found his *radiant*, he was also confounded by how difficult it was to resist his mating instincts. Being completely unhinged wasn't comfortable for him. He practiced control in all things as the king of the Sentinels.

Now, his normal levelheadedness had deserted him completely, his nature demanding that he claim the *radiant* that had been denied him for so long.

He knew he needed to find a way to break their bond quickly. Sophie was an innocent, Zach's sister, and a woman who has been used and abused as an adult. When she was human, her childhood existence had been as miserable as Zach's. She deserved to be free for the first time in her life. The last thing she needed was a demigod Sentinel with a past so dark that she'd never see daylight.

Since the mating of a Sentinel king was unprecedented, he had no idea what it would take to break their bond. Honestly, he didn't know if it was even possible. Although he'd never seen it happen with his Sentinels, he knew it *was* possible for mates to deny each other and live apart, but the bond was never broken. As far as he knew, the two destined mates would yearn for each other for the rest of their lives. But he was determined to try to do this for Sophie. The last thing she needed was a demigod Sentinel with a tainted past. For what he'd done in his past, she'd end up loathing him. Hell, he hated himself, even after all of the years that had passed since he'd changed his life.

*Maybe things are different for a Sentinel king. Maybe the rules are different. Maybe there is a way to break the bond. Things haven't exactly been the same for me and Sophie as it has been for my Sentinels.*

Some things appeared to be the same; some were different. He felt Sophie's lightness in his soul, which was a normal *radiant* reaction, but they were already sharing thoughts and emotions. Hell, they'd been able to communicate before he'd even known who she was back in the Evils' realm.

Taking a deep, calming breath that didn't help worth a damn, Kristoff suggested, "Do you want to see the castle?" He needed time to think, time to plan, and he needed time to figure out what in the hell he was going to do.

"Yes," Sophie answered immediately.

He held out his hand and the fact that Sophie laid her palm on his instantly made him feel like one of the bricks had dropped from the wall he'd built around himself. It was a defense that had worked well for him most of his life; building a mental wall around himself, never letting most emotional things touch him. But her behavior was getting to him, changing him. She trusted him. Even after everything that had happened to her, Sophie put her faith in him without question.

He could feel no hesitation.

He could sense no fear.

*Christ! Can't she identify the darkness that I have inside me?*

"You're the king of the Sentinels," Sophie answered as she squeezed his hand. "You saved my brother's life. I have no reason *not* to trust you."

It was unnerving that Sophie could share his thoughts, just as he could listen to hers.

Honestly, it was downright uncomfortable. Nobody had ever been privy to his personal thoughts unless he wanted them to be. "This *radiant* connection is different," he concluded aloud.

She trotted alongside of him as he strode toward the castle. As they walked, she asked, "How is it different? And I promise I'll try not to invade your mind anymore. But I'm not sure how to stop it."

"It's not your fault," Kristoff assured her, knowing all of this was new to his *radiant*, and his desire to take care of Sophie and protect her jolted him out of his own discomfort. He also wasn't sure if he *wanted* to break the connection they had telepathically. Yeah, it was uncomfortable, but sharing their minds took away the loneliness he'd felt since the day he was born. "It's odd that we've been able to connect telepathically. Generally, a *radiant* doesn't hear her mate's thoughts or feel his emotions until the mating ceremony is over. We've always been able to communicate without words for some reason."

Like Sophie, Kristoff was trying his best not to intrude too far into her thoughts or emotions, although the temptation to know everything about her was difficult to ignore.

"You're the Sentinel king, and a demigod. Maybe that's why it's different," Sophie mused as she climbed the marble stairs to the majestic residence.

She was right. He *was* different, the only one of his kind. The only thing he knew for sure was that his control was slipping fast, and he didn't like it.

He opened the massive entrance with his mind, and power surged through him as he urged Sophie through the enormous door that could only be opened by him or Athena. Entering the grand foyer, power surged through his body, probably a result of being back in the place where he'd been created as the Sentinel king.

*Athena sent me here because she thought I'd be more powerful, strong enough to fight my demon instincts for a while.*

He'd known the goddess long enough to know exactly what she'd been thinking. Unfortunately, being here wasn't helping much. It was the perfect place for security and privacy, but his mating heat was burning hotter every moment he spent in Sophie's company.

"Oh, my God. This place is amazing," Sophie said as she craned her neck to look at the ornately decorated ceiling high above them. "It looks hand painted."

"Athena created it," Kristoff answered, noting that Athena's decorating skills had always been over-the-top.

He smiled as Sophie pulled him from room to room, marveling over the beauty of Athena's palace. Being back in this place was like coming home to him, but for Sophie, it appeared to be like some kind of magical castle, which he guessed was pretty much the truth. He'd just never seen it from the eyes of a human.

When they finally came back downstairs after covering every inch of the upper floor, Kristoff noticed that Sophie was beginning to sway, and he could feel her weariness. "You need to eat," he demanded, irritated with himself for not feeding her earlier.

His mate might seem like a miracle to him, but she *was* human. Food was something she'd never had in abundance, and she was weakened with hunger and malnutrition.

"Do demigods eat?" she asked breathlessly.

He put his arms around her waist and tucked her against him, his demon growling for him to take what belonged to him. He was able to ignore it because his need to take care of her came first. "No. But unlike my fellow Sentinels, I can do this…" A large table appeared with almost every kind of food imaginable in the great hall in front of them. A smaller dining set with chairs was set off to the side of the enormous buffet.

Her eyes wide with amazement and wonder, Kristoff couldn't help but imagine if she'd look like that if he pleasured her body exactly the way he wanted. *Christ!* He wanted, *needed* to stop thinking of her as his mate. Just being near her, watching her, made his whole body pulsate with a need so sharp it was fucking painful.

As they approached the table, she muttered, "It's going to feel strange to eat when you aren't eating."

"I'll eat," he answered readily, not wanting Sophie to ever feel awkward. "It's not that I *don't*. I just don't *have to*. Eating is pleasurable sometimes. I don't have to drink either, but I can appreciate a good Scotch without feeling the effects of the alcohol." Whatever it took to make Sophie feel comfortable, Kristoff vowed he'd do it. Of course, he could think of a lot of things that would please her, all of them carnal in nature.

She looked up at him with a quizzical expression. "I've never eaten for pleasure. Zach and I never had enough food, and they fed me just enough to stay alive in the demon realm."

*Fuck!* Just the thought of Sophie going hungry made Kristoff want to slay every demon who'd deprived her. At that moment, he hated the fact that she'd been hurt and used just because she'd been meant for him.

So much hardship.

So much damn pain.

Sophie had been through so much, yet she still had an innocent sweetness that he wanted to savor. "You'll never be hungry again. I promise you," he vowed fiercely as he led her to the table, handed her a plate, and then watched as she looked at the food with an agonized expression.

"I don't know what to choose," she admitted in a soft, hesitant voice.

Her indecision about something as simple as food turned the knife in his gut again. *Jesus! She's like a child trying to decide on her first candy.*

He forced himself to answer, even though rage was coursing through his body like a runaway train. "Choose anything. Everything. What do you like?"

"I have no idea. I ate whatever scraps I could get for as long as I can remember. When you're hungry, you're grateful for anything edible."

Kristoff forced himself not to let his anger consume him. This wasn't about him; it was about Sophie right now. But dammit, she was his *radiant*. To know that she'd suffered, to feel her hesitation and confusion almost drove him to his breaking point.

He picked up a clean plate and began to pile it high with food. "I'll make you a plate. You can try different things."

What he wanted was for her to eat the whole damn buffet so he could manifest another one. Then she could devour that, too.

The indecision left her expression and she laughed. "Kristoff, I can't possibly eat all that."

He ignored her and grabbed another plate for the desserts after he delivered the first one to the smaller table. "Go sit," he commanded, determined to get one of every sweet on the table. "Eat!" All of the urgency he felt to take care of her needs was in his voice.

Sophie put a hand on his arm. "Stop." She took the dessert plate from his hand and beckoned him over to sit with her. "I'm here. I'm alive. You're feeding me. I'm fine. Come eat with me. Tell me what to try."

Reluctantly, Kristoff stopped gathering food and went to sit across from her, really wanting to go back and fill more plates until they overflowed the dining table.

"Now tell me what all this is," she requested as she picked up a fork and handed one to him.

He shook his head, refusing the utensil. "I can make my own plate. These are all yours."

He pointed out some of his favorite foods on the plate, watching as Sophie closed her eyes in ecstasy every time she tried something new. He tried not to watch, not to imagine the same look on her beautiful face as he drove his cock home inside her over and over again.

But pleasure was pleasure, and he wanted to put that look on her face.

"I'm full," she pronounced after she'd tried a few different foods. "I want to keep eating, but I can't."

She forked a piece of lobster and held it up to him. Startled, he moved back.

"I'm sorry," she said hastily, pulling the fork back quickly. "I just thought you might want some since I can't eat anymore."

She'd been trying to feed *him*?

Kristoff hadn't been sure how to handle that. Nobody had ever really given a damn about whether or not he was content, or if he wanted anything, except Athena. But she'd never tried to feed him. It felt good. It felt…somehow intimate that Sophie was trying to share her food. He hated himself for scaring her off, making her draw back from him. "Give it to me," he insisted.

She hesitated, which made Kristoff hate himself, so he tried to explain. "I'm not used to anyone trying to do something for me. I'm king, and it's my job to take care of everybody else."

She tilted her head and looked at him. "Who takes care of you, then?"

He shrugged. "Nobody. It's my duty to care for my Sentinels and the humans. I'm more powerful."

She smiled at him. "Nobody took care of me in the demon realm, but it feels good now. Can't you just accept the fact that I want to please you because I like you, that I want to share with you?"

Kristoff swallowed hard, touched by the words of the woman across the table from him. Would she still like him if she knew everything about his past? He fucking burned for her, anything she wanted to give him. "Try again. It isn't that I don't like it. I've just never experienced sharing anything with a woman before."

She raised the fork again, and Kristoff didn't hesitate to take the lobster meat from her. "It's good," he proclaimed after he'd swallowed. "But since I don't actually need the food, I'd rather you ate it."

"I had plenty." Sophie put a hand to her flat belly and fed him another piece.

Her capacity to eat much more than a little food at one time was probably small. After near-starvation most of her life, rationally he knew Sophie was full. But he'd feel better if she'd been able to clean both plates.

"You don't like sweets?" he asked curiously as he glanced at the untouched plate.

More than likely she'd never even had something sweet pass between her beautiful lips, so Kristoff took a fork and speared a small piece of chocolate cheesecake. "Try this."

She opened her mouth willingly and took the dessert into her mouth, which had his cock pulsating, his body craving her. He wanted nothing more than to be directly responsible for the orgasmic expression she was making at the moment.

*When the hell did simply eating become an erotic event?*

Everything Sophie did was sensual to him, and he knew she wasn't trying to arouse him. It was his overactive drive to touch her, pleasure her, and bind her to him in the most carnal way possible that was causing his reaction.

He might have more control here at the palace, but his craving to make Sophie his was pounding at his resistance.

A few more bricks of his protective mental wall toppled as he thought about her childhood, about her being cold and hungry in her youth. More fell as he thought about her torture and deprivation in the demon realm.

After feeding her a few more bites of dessert, she held up a hand as she said with a happy laugh, "No more. I'm ready to pop. But it was all amazing."

"So what was your favorite?" he asked curiously, allowing himself to eat the rest of the chocolate cheesecake since Sophie obviously couldn't.

"I think I really liked the seafood. And all of the desserts. Honestly, it's hard to pick a favorite. They were all so wonderful. Thank you. I had no idea food could taste that good."

Kristoff had never heard anybody sound so passionate about food. But then, he'd never seen a woman who had been starved for so many years.

*Never again. Never again. I'll feed her every hour until she's satisfied.*

"Do you think you can ever forget what happened to you in the demon realm?" he asked cautiously.

She looked thoughtful as she answered, "Some things I think will always haunt me. But the pain of Goran's beatings and the horror of him draining my power will fade. After a while, he stopped whipping me into submission because I stopped fighting it and accepted that it was going to happen. I couldn't stop it, and I doubt I'll ever completely forget how it felt to be drained."

Kristoff could feel his protective instincts going on overload as he asked, "Was it bad?" He was so pissed off that he wasn't sure he wanted her answer, but he needed to know.

She nodded. "It hurt like no other wound he inflicted could ever hurt. It felt like every organ in my body was being set on fire by electrical shock, and it seemed like it lasted forever. Eventually, I was able to stop screaming because I knew my pain gave him satisfaction, but it was hard to stay quiet while he kept draining to get every ounce of power he could get. I was always relieved when I finally passed out."

Kristoff lost it. "I planned on killing the bastard anyway, but I'll make it so fucking painful that he'll be screaming for mercy for what he did to you, Sophie." He was breathing hard, his nostrils flaring, every muscle in his body tense with fury. "I can't stand the thought of him hurting you. Christ! I couldn't even deal with the fact that the slimy bastard had laid a finger on you. But knowing how much pain he caused you makes me want to tear him apart piece by piece. He deserves every bit of what he did to you coming back on him."

Sophie's eyes looked bright with moisture as she reached across the table and touched his arm. "Don't. Don't take yourself down to his level. It's over. I didn't know it would upset you or I wouldn't have told you."

"Never keep something like this from me," he demanded in a graveled voice. "If I fail to protect you, if anybody so much as lays a finger on you, you tell me. Understand? I don't want anybody touching you except me, and I promise you that I'll never cause you pain."

Tears flowed down Sophie's face freely as she told him, "Just knowing you care enough to avenge me touches me, Kristoff. It humbles me. Nobody except Zach has ever been my champion. You don't need to harm Goran. The fact that you're willing to do it for me is enough. Thank you for wanting to protect me."

Kristoff gaped at Sophie even as the blind rage continued to pulsate through his body. "Did you think I wouldn't care? Did you think I'd let this go answered?"

"Let it go. I didn't mean to upset you."

"I'm not upset. I'm fucking going ballistic. You're my goddamn *radiant*, and I wasn't there to protect you. That's enough to make any Sentinel crazy. You didn't deserve any of this. You didn't cause anything that happened to you. It's bullshit," he rasped, trying to rein in his anger because he knew it bothered her. "Your life might have been different if you hadn't been tied to a bastard like me."

She spoke of him bringing himself down to Goran's level. Little did she know he'd sunk even lower, and for a much lesser reason than punishing the demon that hurt his *radiant*.

"I would have died as a child," she reminded him. "And I'm free *now*. I don't consider being your radiant as a burden. I consider it an honor that I'll never be worthy of having."

"You wouldn't if you knew about my past," he rumbled. "When I was a demigod, I wasn't a good person."

She shook her head. "It doesn't matter what you were. What matters is who you are now."

Fuck! How he wanted to believe that was true, but she had no idea what she was dealing with.

"Believe it," she said, apparently picking up his thoughts. "I have a lot of things in my past that I feel guilty about. I understand feeling unworthy."

"You could never be unworthy," Kristoff growled.

"Whether I am or not is irrelevant. I felt like I didn't deserve you as my mate."

Kristoff clamped down on his anger as he asked, "And now?"

"Now I'm not sure I'd ever be happy if I didn't at least consider what I'm missing," she told him in a blunt whisper.

He rose and pulled her to her feet. "I promise that I'll provide everything you've missed," he told her gruffly as he pulled her exhausted body against his and cradled her gently.

She sighed and rested her head on his shoulder. "I think I missed this."

Kristoff moved inside her thoughts, shuddering as he realized that what she'd really missed was simple.

For the first time in a long time, Sophie felt like she wasn't alone.

Sadly, knowing that he had to give her up, Kristoff realized that Sophie was what he'd been fucking wanting for so damn long, too. For a moment, he savored the feeling of having her in his arms, knowing that it could never last forever, and absolutely certain that he'd missed this, too.

He wasn't used to tender emotions, but as he held Sophie close, he realized that she wasn't just his radiant anymore. The brave, courageous woman he was comforting was starting to wreak havoc not only with his mind, soul and body, but with his well-shielded heart.

Ignoring the desperate attempt of his demon nature to take over, Kristoff let himself savor the closeness he shared with Sophie, knowing that she'd caused another portion of his wall to drop.

But he didn't give a damn.

She felt so incredibly good in his arms that he couldn't bring himself to even care.

# Chapter Eight

$\mathcal{K}$ ristoff waited until his exhausted mate slept before he transported himself to the demon realm.

Once there, he allowed all of the rage inside him to explode, and it felt so damn good that he immediately sought out and found Goran. There was a violence inside him that wouldn't be denied, all of it caused by the leader of the Evils, the demon who had dared touch and torture his mate.

The minute he appeared in front of Sophie's tormenter, he wasted very little time with words. "You violated my mate. You die now, asshole," Kristoff rasped as he stood in front of the ugly, large, bloody-eyed monster.

"Ah, my wayward prisoner," Goran said in a chilling demon voice. "You're violating our territory."

Kristoff lifted his foot and nailed the demon in the stomach, sending him flying across his putrid bedchamber. Even here where Goran slept, the gore and refuse was everywhere, even on Goran's bed.

"My mate takes precedence before anything else," Kristoff answered with satisfaction as the demon let out a howl of pain as he slammed against the wall.

*Jesus!* How Kristoff wished to draw this out longer, but he also wanted Goran dead before he succumbed to the weaknesses of being in the demon realm.

"But you haven't mated her yet. She's still ripe for the picking," Goran answered as he tried to get back on his feet.

The demon leader's comment sent Kristoff over the edge of sanity. Just the thought of the bastard touching Sophie ever again made his desire to see him dead even more pronounced. He was on Goran before the Evil could even rise, blasting him with bolts of electricity as the demon screeched with pain. "You'll never touch her again because you'll be dead, asshole."

Kristoff could smell the scent of burning demon flesh, and it was the most malodorous scent he'd ever inhaled. But then, he'd never fried an Evil before. Kristoff wanted Sophie's tormentor to feel what it was like to be sizzled with electricity, the same pain that the demon had doled out to Sophie every time he drained her.

*There isn't enough time for me to give him everything Sophie went through.*

His outrage still burning, he began to manifest the sword that would take Goran's head just as the demon lunged for him.

Goran's attack was weak, and Kristoff only traded a few hits with him before he had him under him, pummeling the demons ugly face over and over, unleashing his fury on the piece of shit who had tortured his *radiant*.

Finally, he got around to manifesting his sword, watching the fear on Goran's wrinkled face as it appeared in his hand and over the demon lord's head.

"How does it feel to be on the other side of pain?" Kristoff asked furiously. "Feel good to you? 'Cause it feels fucking fantastic to me." Even though his central anger was still about Sophie, he hadn't forgotten Goran's mind fuck or his torture while he was his prisoner.

Real fear appeared in Goran's red-eyed expression as Kristoff held the weapon that would take the demon's head. "Don't kill me. I didn't kill your mate," Goran begged.

"Only because you couldn't and didn't want to. She always recharged so you could hurt her again."

"I-I didn't kill you either," Goran stammered, his red eyes riveted to the large blade over his head.

"Because you wanted to keep me barely alive for insurance. Otherwise, I'd be dead right now."

Kristoff was insane with the desire to make this creature pay for everything he'd done to Sophie, but he knew he was running out of time.

"T-that's not t-true," Goran stuttered.

"Bullshit!" Kristoff lowered the blade to Goran's neck. "You liked it. You get off on causing others pain. You wanted more power. You even killed other *radiants* for what you could get from them."

His rage still relentlessly driving him, Kristoff lifted the sword to end Goran's pathetic life.

It was on his lethal, downward stroke that Kristoff was stopped by a power greater than his own, his death blow stopped only a few inches from Goran's neck.

"You can't kill him, Kristoff."

*Athena. What in the hell was she doing here?*

"Don't interfere," he warned. "He deserves to die for what he did to Sophie and the other *radiants.*"

"I agree completely," Athena said calmly as she approached and dragged Kristoff from Goran. "But unfortunately, he *has* to live. Both of you are critical to the balance." Athena glanced at Goran with a look of loathing as she warned, "Remember my words. You're lucky Kristoff didn't die. You may not have to follow all of the rules of the gods anymore, but his death by an Evil's hand will end all of you."

Kristoff shrugged her off as he watched Goran try to get to his feet as he asked, "What? Why?"

Athena shrugged. "I didn't make up the rules. They were set by prophecies the gods wrote, and you both need to stay alive. If you kill him, you endanger the Sentinels and humanity. If Goran kills you, the Evils and their realm will cease to exist."

Kristoff's fist tightened on the sword, his need to obliterate Goran forever still pounding at him. But in the end, he knew he was fucked, and not in a good way. His vow to lead his men and protect the human world would always win.

"So I can really never kill him either?" Goran asked as he finally rose, supporting himself against the wall.

"Nope. Not unless you're feeling suicidal," Athena answered. "Come, Kristoff. We have to go."

"How did you get here?" he asked Athena, still clutching his sword tightly.

"I can get here alone, but I can't lead others in like Kat does."

Kristoff eyed Goran angrily. "Is there any rule that I can't hurt him badly?"

"No," Athena answered cheerfully. "Just don't lop off his head."

Kristoff stepped forward and wielded his sword, nailing Goran right beneath his chest with his blade. Yanking his sword free, he took another shot at him. And then another. Every impalement lessened his desire for vengeance as he watched Goran gasp and slide down the wall and land on the filthy floor, unconscious.

Once the demon leader was down, he dropped the blade on top of Goran's lifeless body, knowing it would take a very long time for him to recover.

"That will have to be enough," Kristoff informed Athena calmly.

"Enough? You just kicked his ass. He won't recover for months."

"I wanted him dead," he grumbled.

"I know. I wish I could have given you the satisfaction. But I can't," Athena replied sadly.

He nodded abruptly to signal that he understood, then he waited for the goddess to disappear before he followed her out of the demon realm, leaving Goran critically wounded on the floor without a second thought.

The next evening, Sophie sat beside Kristoff on his bed, watching as he finally fell into a healing sleep.

His punishment for entering the demon realm had been swift, excruciating for her to watch, and devastating because she knew he'd gone there without a thought to the side effects he'd suffer.

She hadn't left his side since Athena had brought him home, spilling the story of what Kristoff had done, and how disappointed he was that Goran couldn't die.

Sophie moved to lie down next to him now that he was no longer thrashing and in the throes of a reaction to entering the demon realm and harming Goran so badly that he would be out of commission for quite some time.

Lying face to face with him, she reached out and stroked his whiskered jaw as she whispered, "Why would you do this to yourself. Why?"

"Because you're my mate," Kristoff grumbled, still half asleep.

Sophie hadn't expected an answer, and as she probed his mind slightly, she could feel that he was somewhere between sleep and awareness. "They could have killed you. Goran could have killed you."

"He needed to die. As long as we aren't mated, you're still vulnerable. He could come after you again," Kristoff replied in a groggy voice. "I don't want him to ever touch you again."

Sophie felt her heart in her throat as she bit her lip to keep from sobbing. Having someone fight for her was so foreign to her, but it touched her more than Kristoff could ever know. He'd risked his life for her safety without a second thought.

"I don't want you hurt, either," she whispered back to him, pushing a lock of hair back from his forehead. "Promise me you won't do something like that again. I can't stand to see you pay for breaking the rules."

"Fuck the rules," Kristoff rasped. "I've followed the rules forever. When it comes to you, I'll break every damn rule ever written to save you."

A tear trickled down her cheek. As far as she knew, Kristoff kept a tight rein on his Sentinels, and he led by example. He never broke the rules. "How did you even manage to do it? You're bound by the rules."

"You're more important to me, the only thing that's been stronger than my compulsion to follow the dictates of the Sentinel laws," he muttered hoarsely. "You make me crazy," he added earnestly.

Sophie's heart skipped a beat as she found herself suddenly staring into his beautiful eyes as they fluttered open.

She answered quietly, "It broke my heart to see you hurting because of me."

Their eyes locked and held, and Sophie couldn't pull her gaze away from the intensity reflected in Kristoff's gaze. "You're mine. My precious mate. Do you really think there's nothing I wouldn't do to make you happy, to keep you safe?"

Sophie could still feel the lump in her throat as she replied, "I think I'm starting to get the message." Really, she was starting to understand that Kristoff was unstoppable when it came to his protective instincts.

"Being in my bed puts you in a dangerous position," he told her gruffly.

Her core clenched in response, and her nipples peaked to an almost painful hardness. The look in Kristoff's eyes wasn't amber. Sophie knew he wasn't at full strength yet, but the intense, fierce desire he had for her showed in his tumultuous stare.

She smiled at him. "I hardly think you're in any position to do anything about it."

"You think not?" he growled as he rolled her over and pinned her beneath him. "My cock is always ready to be buried inside you. My body is always ready to fuck you into next week. Don't underestimate how much I need you, Sophie. It could get you into trouble."

Her heart was hammering so loud that she could hear it *whooshing* in her ears. In a matter of seconds, he had her body trembling with a need so sharp it was almost painful. "Don't," she whispered. "You're still recovering. Please."

"Fuck! I can't take much more," Kristoff rumbled.

"Kiss me," she asked impulsively, needing to feel the warmth of his body on top of hers for a little longer.

"Playing with fire," Kristoff uttered as his tortured gaze swept over her face.

Sophie freed her arms from the weight of his body and speared her hands through his hair. Her desperation to feel him overwhelmed her and she urged his head down.

Kristoff completed the descent, capturing her mouth with a tortured groan. He plundered until Sophie could do nothing except respond with the same desperation that Kristoff was experiencing, clinging to him like she never wanted to let go.

He explored.

He tasted.

He possessed.

Sophie felt his compulsion to claim her, and the need echoed back to her, making her moan against his mouth and lower her hand to claw at his back even as she rationally knew they had to end the embrace before they both went up in flames.

*Stop!*

She sent him the mental message even as she clung to him, sending him mixed signals.

Kristoff grunted as he yanked his mouth from hers like it was painful, which for Sophie, it really was.

He rolled onto his back, his fists clenched and his body tense. Sophie could see the ripple of every muscle as he held back his desire.

"I'm sorry," she told him breathlessly. "I knew you were still recovering. I shouldn't have asked you to do that."

"I'm never going to let an invitation to touch you pass. I'd have to be dead," Kristoff replied, his voice strained.

"You need sleep, Kristoff."

"I. Need. You." His graveled voice was quieter as he closed his eyes.

"No one has ever needed me before," she confessed, her voice tremulous. Her body was still trying to calm after Kristoff's unexpected burst of strength.

"I fucking need you enough to make up for everyone who never did," he grumbled unhappily.

"You're in my mind," Sophie reminded him. "You know I want you, too. So much it's almost uncontrollable." Which was why she'd asked him to kiss her when she really shouldn't have. Her urges were becoming hard to ignore.

"I know," Kristoff acknowledged. "I can also sense that you're exhausted."

"I haven't slept since Athena brought you home. I couldn't. You were in so much pain."

"It was nothing. I've suffered much worse punishment. And I'm fine now. Sleep, Sophie. Stay here with me. It might kill me to know you're here, but it's worse when you aren't."

She felt exactly the same way, so she made herself comfortable next to him, her body starting to feel the strain of sleep deprivation.

"You haven't promised me that you won't do something crazy just to protect me again," she reminded him sleepily.

"No, I didn't. Nor will I. I take my vows seriously, and I can't tell you that I'd never do anything to keep you safe, because I will."

"Stubborn Sentinel," she admonished.

"Stubborn mate," he answered drowsily. "Accept that I'm always going to do whatever it takes to make you happy and make sure you're safe."

As she fell asleep without answering, Sophie smiled. Kristoff gave a new meaning to bossy, but he was doing it to try to keep her safe.

Since it felt so good to be cherished, she was pretty sure she could live with his demanding nature. In fact, the more she came to understand his motivations, she knew she could.

# Chapter Nine

Sophie spent the next two weeks catching up on everything she'd missed in the last few centuries. To say she'd been shocked at first was putting it mildly. Kristoff had taken her to her native London, and there was very little she recognized anymore. Some buildings had been preserved, but were used for other purposes now. Very little had remained of the city she'd known two centuries ago, except the pain she and Zach had experienced when they were two children trying to survive in a very cold, very brutal world. *That* she remembered. *That* she couldn't forget. But seeing how the world had moved on and progressed had helped.

They traveled somewhere new every day, but they always returned to Athena's castle, where Kristoff continued to feed her more than she could eat, got even more protective and possessive about her being his *radiant*, but never mentioned what they were going to do about that issue.

He treated her well. Actually, he was almost *too* polite. Sophie shared his thoughts, experienced his desperation like it was her own. Or was it her own? She was getting to the point where she couldn't tell.

*Maybe he decided he doesn't want me anymore. Maybe he finally realized that my pox marks and scars are ugly.*

Instantly, she knew that her negative thoughts were her own insecurities. Kristoff didn't see her as an ignorant, scarred mate. That wasn't the problem. Although she tried not to intrude, she could sense his need, his desperation to claim *her*. *His radiant.* He didn't even seem to notice her faults. Sometimes, her attraction to him overwhelmed her, and it was usually because his emotions were getting so entangled with her own.

She sat outside on the beach, mesmerized by the magical, deep-blue cascade of waves as they hit the sand over and over again, trying to figure out what was *really* going on with Kristoff. Rarely did he lock his thoughts from her, but there were things behind a mental door that occasionally slammed shut when he was contemplating something he didn't want her to know.

Sophie wasn't quite sure if he closed her off intentionally, or if it was subconscious, but she could feel the distance when it happened, and it hurt to the depths of her soul.

Being destined mates was complicated. It was as though they were connected, and when she was excluded, it was almost physically painful, a deep ache that wouldn't go away.

He hadn't touched her since the night he'd recovered from being in the demon realm to attempt to slay Goran, but she knew he *wanted* to, and his emotions were almost violent, frantic and frenzied, as he painfully tried to hold himself back.

*Why? Why is he checking himself when it's hurting him?*

Letting the sand sift between her toes as she moved her bare feet, Sophie decided she'd take things as they happened. Problem was, she really wanted *something* to occur, and she definitely wanted to know exactly what Kristoff was thinking. Most of the time, he communicated openly, mostly sharing information with her, and talking about memories of Zach and Athena.

*But he never talks about his life before he became the Sentinel king.*

Sophie assumed whatever had happened, it wasn't good. But she was his mate, and she knew he was close to the edge. She could *feel* it in her soul.

Athena didn't think Kristoff could survive not mating.

However, Kristoff was determined *not* to mate, even though Sophie knew ignoring his instincts was practically killing him.

How could the situation be resolved?

Her confidence was growing as Kristoff showed her more and more of the world as it was now. So much had changed, but some things remained the same. There was a lot of amazing technology in the world today, but still too many people were still struggling just to survive.

*Just like Zach and I did two centuries ago.*

She swept her sandy hands over her blue jeans, shivering as she thought about the way Kristoff had looked at her as she'd left the castle in only denims and a T-shirt. His eyes had been amber, his expression somber, his gaze practically burning her alive as he watched her leave, looking like he wanted nothing more than to go with her, even though he'd refused with a simple shake of his head when she'd asked him if he wanted to join her. It couldn't be the fact that he disapproved of her attire. After all, he'd been the one to create her clothing for her, helping her catch up on what women wore these days. Although it had taken her a while to get used to wearing pants, she had to admit that it was one of the changes she was learning to embrace.

"Hello, Sophie."

The greeting came so abruptly from behind her that she startled, even though she recognized Athena's voice.

Scrambling to get up to greet her visitor, she plopped back down when the goddess motioned for her to stay where she was, and then joined her on the sand.

"Athena. What are doing here?" Sophie realized what a dumb question she'd asked considering this was Athena's dimension, her creation, and her home. "That was a stupid question. This is your place."

The blonde woman shook her head as she positioned herself comfortably in the sand. Dressed much like Sophie, the goddess still radiated a power that was slightly intimidating. "I wanted to see how you were doing here. This isn't my home anymore. I haven't even been here for a very long time. Maybe I was more at peace here, but I was still lonely. Home is wherever Hunter is now."

The peaceful look and small, contented smile on Athena's face told Sophie that this was a place the goddess didn't need anymore. "Kristoff has been reintroducing me to the world. In so many ways it's changed, but fundamentally, it really isn't that different."

Athena nodded. "That's how I felt, and my life dates back thousands of years. People are still the same: some good, some bad. There's still war and battles, different cultures and people fighting over what's right and what's wrong. Prejudice and bias still exists, but more cloaked in what humans consider a more civilized manner." She snorted as she let out a mocking laugh. "But I have to admit, I would rather be in the world I have today than anywhere else. Technology is a wonderful thing. I won't complain about that."

Sophie watched the beautiful blonde tilt her head toward the sun as she asked her, "What news is there about the Evils. How is the cleanup going?"

"Time doesn't pass quite the same here as it does in the human realm. Barely a few days have gone by there, and trying to right all of the wrongs the Evils did will take time. But we'll get it taken care of." She hesitated before mentioning, "You and Kristoff haven't mated."

"How did you know?" Sophie asked curiously. Then, remembering Athena was a goddess who knew a lot of things without asking, she continued, "No. He's been more of a teacher and mentor to me."

"He's meant to be your mate, Sophie. And I can tell because I can still feel the slight unbalance. Everything that should be done hasn't happened. I'm Kristoff's Sentinel creator, and we're closely tied. I can still feel the echo of his sorrow...and yours. It's always been present with Kristoff, and now I feel it even stronger because you two are connected."

Sophie finally gave up hiding anything from Athena and her probing stare. Strangely, she wasn't intimidated by the goddess anymore. Seeing how much Athena adored Hunter, and how much she cared about Kristoff's happiness had melted away most of her hesitation.

"He refuses to bond me to him. He says no woman deserves that fate, especially not me. I think he's trying to figure out a way to reverse the *radiant* thing." She sighed as she added her biggest concern, "It's getting painful. I ache so badly that I feel irritable and restless. Is it the same for Kristoff?"

Athena snorted. "It's a thousand times worse than what you're feeling. Stubborn male! The mating bond is irreversible. You can deny him, and he can deny you, but you'll still be his *radiant*. And I don't think he can survive the strength of his attraction. You're the part of him that he's been missing for so long, the woman he desperately needs to stop the emptiness that's been plaguing him for eons. Because he's the king and a demigod instead of a human, his urge to obey the command of the gods is stronger, more powerful than any of his previously human Sentinels."

"I'm not sure what to do," Sophie admitted. "I mean, both of us were pretty much thrown into this situation without even knowing each other, but it's worse now that I've gotten to know how kind he is, how much he's sacrificed himself for his Sentinels. He'd die for any of them." She hesitated before adding, "He's willing to die for me." She sighed as she continued, "Kristoff mentioned that our mating situation is unusual, but I don't know how it works normally, so I have nothing to compare it to. You, Talia and Kat shared your experiences, but what exactly *are* the rules? How is it supposed to work for a normal Sentinel?"

Athena quickly laid out the basics of how the *radiant* mating generally occurred, providing her with information about how it had been different with her and Hunter because she was a goddess. When she finished, she asked quietly, "What do *you* want, Sophie? Do you want to be with Kristoff?"

She shook her head but answered, "I don't know. I guess..." her voice trailed off.

Athena glanced at her questioningly. "What is it?"

"I have feelings for him, things that aren't part of the mating bond. I care for him in ways other than just as my destined mate. The overwhelming desire is there, but I want...more. I want somebody to love me. I don't want just an arranged mating. Maybe that sounds stupid since me being handed a Sentinel like Kristoff is absurd in the first place. He's too rich, too handsome, too powerful for me." She spilled out everything, all of her emotions in her voice, and choked back a sob.

Truly, what Sophie wanted was somebody who loved *her*, a man that wanted *her*. Sadly, she realized that she *did* want that somebody to be Kristoff.

Sophie finally confessed, "I'm falling in love with him. My heart aches. It's not just my soul and my body that wants him anymore."

Athena's face softened and she reached out and pulled Sophie into her arms and hugged her, rocking her like a mother would a child. "I'm sorry. I forget how little you know of the Sentinels or any other world except being a captive of the Evils. Of course you don't understand."

The friendly comforting from Athena made Sophie break, and she sobbed out her fear, pain, and every negative emotion she had, feelings that had been bottled up inside her for longer than she could remember. Things she'd thought she'd hidden rose up and left her helpless to a flow of painful wails as Athena held onto her tightly and let her exhaust herself.

"Everything will work out," Athena crooned patiently. "I doubt you'll ever forget the torture you had to endure, but it will fade. I promise it will."

She clutched Athena like she was her lifeline, trying to absorb the goddess's gentle confidence. She'd never felt the peace of being comforted by a female friend or relative. Her and Zach had been orphans trying to survive as children, and after that, all she'd ever known was scorn, torture and pain. As her sobs subsided, she confessed, "The worst part was watching the women come and go, knowing they were all going to die and I would probably eventually wake up alone. That was always the way it happened. Over and over again. I felt guilty because I was the only one who survived when I would have been glad if I'd never woken up again. Some of the women were there long enough to be my friends."

It was as if a lifetime of anguish was suddenly breaking loose from her soul, finally free to escape.

Athena let out an angry exclamation as she rubbed Sophie's back. "It wasn't your fault. None of it was ever your fault. The gods are assholes sometimes. What you went through wasn't a test. It was an atrocity."

Sophie finally untangled herself from Athena and swiped at her tears. "I'm sorry. I don't usually let go like that. I never wanted the Evils to know their torture worked. I refused to let them see how much it really ate me alive when those women were killed."

The goddess grasped Sophie by the shoulders gently. "You're among friends now, Sophie. It will take time for you to adjust to that."

Sophie composed herself and looked at Athena. "You asked me what I wanted? I guess I just want Kristoff to love me for me, and not because I'm his *radiant*."

"Even though the gods can be cruel, you'd never be mated with someone who could never love you, and vice versa. The attraction might start because you're Kristoff's *radiant*, so the primitive needs come first. But eventually they all get tangled up with love and tender emotions. It's the most amazing feeling in the world," Athena confided with a smile.

"I think I already care about him too much," Sophie confessed, feeling nothing but exhausted relief from pouring her soul out to Athena.

"He deserves it, even though he feels he doesn't. His life wasn't easy before he became a Sentinel. He didn't feel like he belonged anywhere. Not in the human world, and he paid a very high price for entering the world of the gods," Athena told her solemnly.

"What?" Sophie asked curiously.

Athena shrugged. "It isn't my story to tell. But I somehow don't think you'd judge him too harshly."

"How could I? He's been nothing but good to me," Sophie answered, confused.

"He has his own insecurities and sadness," Athena said in a warning voice. "But he needs to let go of the past and embrace his future."

"How can I help him?" Sophie asked breathlessly, knowing she'd do anything to help her mate. She craved him just as much as he wanted her. If she had to take the first giant leap of faith in him, she'd do it.

*I'm done holding back my emotions because I'm insecure!*

Athena smiled as she rose to her feet. "Love him," she answered quietly. "Make him believe he deserves to be happy. Share thoughts and feelings with him. Follow your instincts. Follow your heart instead of your head."

Sophie nodded, the ever-increasingly strength of ache for the Sentinel king who thought he deserved nothing except to serve squeezing her heart. She didn't know why he felt the way he did, and she wasn't going to try to probe the thoughts from his head. Kristoff needed to trust her enough to share his secrets.

"Take care of him. He's hurting right now," Athena advised.

A moment later, the goddess disappeared like she'd never been there on the beach.

All Sophie could hear was the crashing of the waves methodically hitting the sand.

She stood up and brushed the sand off herself with determination.

*Enough of polite conversation.* She ached desperately to know Kristoff intimately, and in so many ways. Now that she was acquainted with the new world she'd live in, she was ready to take on the challenge of somehow getting closer to her intended mate, whether he wanted it or not.

Sophie intended to break down the walls Kristoff had erected, expose the pain he'd hidden away for so long, and erase it with showing him just how much she cared.

As she walked back to the palace, her body was already responding with the anticipation of seeing her handsome, brooding Sentinel again. Her nipples hardened to diamond-like peaks, and her core clenched viciously as she thought about how much she wanted him to teach her what it was like to be sexually satisfied. She had no doubt Kristoff was the only one who could.

She was ready to stop denying that she wanted him. Her carnal desire for Kristoff had just grown stronger and stronger.

*If he's feeling the same thing multiplied by a thousand, he has to be half out of his mind by now.*

Sophie's heart rate accelerated as she got closer to the grand home in front of her. She was determined to help her Sentinel in any way possible, but he'd probably try to block her.

*Then I'll just hammer away at his barriers. He needs me right now.*

Strangely, the fact that Kristoff's happiness was basically in her hands didn't bother her nearly as much as it did before.

She'd make him happy, and she wouldn't stop until his desperation and sadness was a thing of the past.

Neither of them needed to suffer anymore, and she was more than ready to move on and share less painful, more ecstasy-filled days and nights with her mate.

# Chapter Ten

ophie's courage almost disappeared when she found Kristoff sitting in the massive library of the palace reading through ancient tombs. He was grumbling to himself, obviously in an impatient, mercurial mood.

*It doesn't matter how bold I have to be. He's in pain. I can feel it. And I'm the woman who can stop it.*

Straightening her spine, she walked into the massive chamber filled from the floor to a massively high ceiling with magical books. "What are you looking for?" she asked curiously as she approached the large oak desk where he was seated.

Kristoff barely looked up. "Answers. I have to find some fucking information." He slammed the tomb in front of him closed so loudly that the sound reverberated through the spacious room. "What good are so many books when I can't find what I'm looking for?" he asked angrily, obviously frustrated.

"What do you want?" she asked as she slowly fingered the spines of some of the books near the desk. "I think books must be wonderful. I never learned to read."

"You want to read?" Kristoff asked, staring at her now.

"Of course. I'd love to know what adventures are in these books." Sophie turned around to look at him.

Kristoff scowled. "Zach couldn't read either. Neither one of you ever went to school."

Sophie shrugged. "There was no way for us to go. And just surviving was nearly impossible. How did Zach learn? Did you teach him?"

She watched Kristoff struggle to keep his eyes from turning amber. It was an action she'd become accustomed to, and that she could spot almost immediately. His brows drew closer together, the effort showing in his expression. His exertion was almost a palpable tension in the room.

Kristoff rose, his height intimidating to a woman of her smaller stature. He moved toward her, stopping right in front of her. Dropping his large hand on her head, Sophie could feel the warmth of his touch permeating her mind, but she didn't move. She knew that Kristoff would never hurt her, and she trusted him completely.

He backed off immediately, the moment he lifted his palm from her hair, then went and sat back down at the desk. "Pick a book. It's easier to just give you the skill than to take the time to learn it. It's something you should have had a long time ago."

It took her a moment to understand his meaning, but the moment she understood what he'd done, she yanked a book from the shelf, and opened it. Her mouth dropped open in astonishment as she realized she could understand every word written on the first page. "I can read," she whispered huskily. "Oh, my God. Kristoff! I can read."

"Of course you can. I just gave you the skill," Kristoff answered gruffly.

She started reading aloud from the classic fiction book she was holding, her heart pounding as she breezed through the first paragraph. Finally, she closed the book carefully, put it back in its place on the shelf and turned back to Kristoff.

Her teacher was smirking as she blinked at him in surprise. "You can do that? You can just give me knowledge?"

"You just read that passage, didn't you? I still have the powers of a demigod. I gave Zach his ability to read, too. As I remember, he spent weeks in my library once he was actually able to enjoy books."

His smile became softer as he talked about Zach as a young man. "Of course, that was before television."

"I'm sure he still likes to read. There's something much more intimate about reading," Sophie considered. "I think because even though lots of people have read the book, I would think it would be more personal."

Kristoff nodded. "It is. It's much more solitary, and it gives you time to interpret the story in your own way from your own experiences in life. Much of this collection is ancient, but it's automatically updated through the years with a lot of the classics."

She shook her head, amazed that books had been added for eons without anyone ever being here.

"Athena loves books," Kristoff added. "She created a library equal to this one at the mansion where she was imprisoned."

Sophie shuddered, already knowing that the beautiful blonde goddess had been completely alone except for Kristoff for thousands of years. Two centuries had seemed like eternity to Sophie. She could only imagine how lonely Athena had been.

"If you have the power, why didn't you just bring me up to date this way?" Why had he bothered to take her everywhere, show her things as they were now?

He shrugged. "Some things have to be experienced. Knowing has to be done in person. It makes us who we are. Skills can be given without messing with your spirit and understanding of the things around you."

Moving forward, she impulsively laid her palm on his lightly whiskered jaw and looked down at him solemnly. "Thank you," she said gratefully. "You've given me a priceless gift. I was planning on learning. But what you've done will open up a whole new world of information for me immediately."

A low rumble came from his throat, and his eyes immediately flashed to amber as he reached up and gripped the hand she was using to cup his jaw. "It was nothing," he snapped in an animalistic growl.

Sophie knew his control was slowly eroding, his battle to stay stable causing him an enormous amount of agony.

"I know so little, Kristoff. Everything you've given me, done for me, and shown me is something I'll never forget. It wasn't nothing to me." She hesitated as his grip on her hand grew tighter, not because she was afraid, but because she needed to know how far she could push him. "You were searching for a way to reverse the mating link?" she asked grimly. "You're hurting badly. I can sense it."

"Christ! I try to lock my damn pain away from you, keep it far from your mind. It's not working?" he asked huskily as he stood up and pinned her with a needy gaze that was no longer hiding what he was experiencing.

I have to convince him. I have to make him understand that there's no reason for him to put himself through this anymore. His protective instincts included guarding her from his emotions, and it was no longer necessary.

She nodded slowly. "It works, but I can still sense how you feel." She didn't mention the fact that her own needs were getting unbearable. Like him, she'd tried to shield them by not voicing or reacting to the throbbing anguish she was experiencing, a pain that just got greater every day.

"I have to find a way to finish this!" he said gruffly. "You don't really need me anymore, and you deserve to have the life you never experienced. The only thing I fucking deserve is to be the Sentinel king because I've earned that right through service to the Sentinels. But I can't be a decent mate to you. I wasn't a good man when I was a demigod, Sophie. I was nothing but evil, and serving for Athena was a privilege."

Sophie knew he was trying to protect her, but why did she need protection from him? Her heart melted as she looked up at his tortured expression.

*He really believes he deserves nothing good. He really believes that his long-ago past defines him still. He'd sacrifice all just to keep from hurting me. Like he'd ever hurt me? Does he really believe he would?*

Sophie didn't buy it for a second. No matter how fierce and dangerous he appeared when he was in the throes of his mating agony, he was still...Kristoff.

Heat flooded between her thighs as she watched the muscle in his jaw twitch. Kristoff was physical perfection, but more than that, everything about him fascinated her. He was a mystery she hadn't quite solved, but her attraction and affection for him was incredibly real.

Her soul cried out at the thought of not being near him anymore. And her heart began to weep.

"You're still determined to separate us then?" she asked huskily.

He nodded. "Yeah. I'm not sure how I'll manage it since there appears to be no way out for us. I could put distance between us, but I know I'd be hunting you down the moment you were gone. I would follow you anywhere you go. I wouldn't be able to stop myself."

"Why?" she asked, her voice trembling slightly.

Sophie didn't want the mating bond between them dissolved anymore. The barrage of emotions she was feeling for this stubborn, fierce but tender Sentinel king were all too complicated. Emotions from her heart, soul and body were all confused, but she knew exactly what she wanted.

*Kristoff.*

In some ways, it didn't matter why she felt the way she did, that she sometimes had a hard time separating her own emotions from their bond. She knew that her body wouldn't respond to him this strongly if she hadn't come to love and respect this complicated god/Sentinel who was looking at her like he wanted to devour her.

*Me? Scarred ugly duckling? He wants me?*

She was still amazed that Kristoff saw her way differently than most people probably would. To human men, she'd be forever a scarred mess. To Kristoff, she was his greatest desire.

Now, he was *her* greatest desire, too, and there was nothing she could do to keep her body from reacting, her nipples hardening almost to the point of being painful.

The tension grew in the room as her question about why he wanted to separate them went unanswered.

His nostrils flared and his body was tense as he backed her up against the wall of books and simply…stared.

"Why?" she repeated breathlessly as her heart raced erratically. "Why are you trying so hard to avoid something that's so natural for a Sentinel?"

His body crowded her, his hands slamming down on the bookshelves on both sides of her head, effectively trapping her. Not that she was able to move. At the moment, he had her mesmerized with his mercurial, agony-filled gaze.

"Do you have any idea how badly I want to fuck you, Sophie?" he asked roughly.

She shook her head, fascinated by the graveled need she could hear in his voice.

"I want to bury myself inside you. I want to see you wearing my mark. Mine. I want to know that you belong to me. I think I'd kill any other man that even touched you right now, and no matter how hard I try, I don't think I can give you up. This feeling, this inherent desire to own you is relentless, selfish. But I'm losing all ability to give a damn about that. You don't deserve to be with me. I've done things I can never forgive myself for doing, much less expect you to forgive me. I'm. Not. Good. For. You." The last sentence left Kristoff's lips as though he was straining to say the words.

"What you've done in the past doesn't matter," Sophie answered empathically. All that mattered was *right now*. Kristoff was a good man, the best she'd ever known other than Zach. Granted, she hadn't really known that many that weren't Evils, but she'd encountered a lot of mean men as a child.

"It matters!" Kristoff's voice was powerful and anguished as he replied.

"Then forget about the mating…for now. Can't you just fuck me?" The words left her mouth before she could stop them, her body craving Kristoff so desperately that she couldn't keep from speaking what she felt. "If you're going to somehow ignore our bond, I want to feel what it's like to have you inside me first. I want to know... pleasure."

The Evils had defiled her, clawed her and hurt her, but they weren't actually able to rape her since they didn't have the necessary equipment to do so.

*Once!* Just one time she wanted to know the pleasure a woman could experience with a man she desired. And the only man she'd ever wanted was this intense, complicated, god-like handsome man who was holding her against him like he couldn't bear to let her go.

"Oh, Jesus. Sophie. You have no idea what you're asking for." Kristoff groaned as he threaded his hands through her hair and slammed his mouth down on hers.

Instantly, the moment he repositioned his hands so she could move, Sophie wrapped her arms around his muscular shoulders, savoring the warmth and strength of his hard, heated body. Her hands speared through his course hair, and she shivered at the decadent feeling of the thick strands between her fingers.

He tilted her head back, demanding deeper access to her mouth, his tongue sweeping into the cavern like it was his and always would be.

Sophie's body burned with an incendiary heat that she'd never experienced before, and she moaned against his lips, entangling his tongue with hers in an effort to get closer to him.

But it didn't satiate the burning hunger she had.

She needed Kristoff inside her.

She needed him to make her part of him.

She needed everything he could give her and more.

When he finally lifted his mouth, they were both panting. Sophie could feel the tension in his body. "Please, don't stop." Sensing he was fighting with himself, she pleaded, "Please. I'm not asking you to make me your *radiant* forever. I just want to feel this kind of pleasure for a little bit longer."

"You really don't know what you're asking for," Kristoff admonished in a low, feral reply.

"Maybe I don't. But I want you." It really was that simple. Her every need was dependent on Kristoff right at the moment.

He backed away, his eyes burning into her with a crazed expression. "Go. Leave. I can't do this. Escape now while you can."

"I don't want to escape," she protested.

He held up his hand. "Go!"

Sophie's head started to spin, and then, as she gave Kristoff a pleading look, everything faded to darkness for a moment before she landed in the bedroom Kristoff had given her to use.

As irritated as he had been, he'd dropped her softly on the bed, as far away from him as she could get without leaving the house.

Heart, body and soul, she hurt from the abrupt separation. She panted, her heart racing as she took a few minutes to catch her breath.

Kristoff had sent her away.

*Did he finally realize that I'm scarred and hideous?*

Maybe he wanted her because the *radiant* bond was there. Maybe he was being forced into wanting her, but personally found her undesirable. Maybe just giving each other pleasure wasn't possible.

Her confusion bombarding her, Sophie couldn't figure out why Kristoff had sent her away. She'd offered herself up to him on a silver platter without any strings attached.

And he'd rejected her, sent her away from him.

A tear trickled down her cheek, meandering its way to her chin.

She swiped it away, realizing although her body cried out for Kristoff, right now the thing that ached the most was her heart.

Kristoff had whisked himself from the library to the shower, a task he never needed to perform. But it was the best way to get himself off, or try to anyway.

He leaned his forehead against the ceramic tile and pumped on his steely cock so forcefully that it was becoming raw and painful.

Warm water pounded against his back, but he didn't notice it.

He was too desperate, too raw, too fucking crazed to care.

He'd been trying to jack off since the day he met his *radiant*, and it very seldom worked. Nothing could replace the mating heat coursing through his body and his soul.

*Can't you just fuck me. I want to experience pleasure.*

Her words echoed through his mind until he was pounding his cock, allowing himself to think about what it would be like to pin his mate against a wall and bury himself inside her.

The heat.

The wetness.

The fucking incredible feel of her tight pussy clamping around him, claiming him just as surely as he'd claim her.

"I need her," he rasped, letting his imagination run wild with visions of providing her the pleasure she so desired.

*I'd satisfy her until she was so sated she couldn't move.*

Visions of burying his head between her thighs and swirling his tongue along her slick, pink flesh while she screamed his name in a powerful climax made him stroke harder, faster.

Imagining her taking his cock between her lush, sexy lips sent him over the edge, and he finally released himself against the tile of the shower with an agonized groan.

Dropping to his knees, he shuddered, his release giving him very little relief from the fantasies that he wanted to be reality.

*Mine. She's fucking mine and I can't claim her.*

He wasn't sure how long he knelt in the shower, his fists clenched, his body consumed by fire, his will near the breaking point.

As the water turned cold, he dried himself with his magic and turned off the water. Tired of being engaged in the most difficult battle he'd ever fought, he settled himself in his bed, still fighting the desire to connect with Sophie.

# Chapter Eleven

ophie walked carefully through the fog, not quite sure where she was or what she was doing trying to fight her way through a fluffy, white substance that was barely permeable. Her hands in front of her, she struggled to break free of the blinding, heavy vapor that was obscuring her vision.

Finally, she stepped into the light, leaving the darkness behind her, and it took her a minute to focus. When she did, she let out a startled scream as she saw what looked like an animal cage, a space so small that the large body inside it was rolled into a ball to fit inside the prison.

Still, she recognized Kristoff. Rushing forward, she could only get within a few feet of his prison before her feet stopped and stuck to the ground, her body paralyzed in place.

"Kristoff," she panted urgently.

He was alive, his animalistic, blue-eyed stare as cold as the Arctic in the winter. It was obvious that he didn't recognize her. Sophie didn't think he even knew she was there.

"Please," she begged aloud to nobody in particular, needing to get to him.

Although he was recognizable to her, his golden hair was shaven, and his naked, trembling body was covered in blood and scars. The heavy breaths leaving his body were audible, his pain apparent.

*How long had he been crammed into his tiny prison? It had to hurt to be unable to move, his body twisted like a pretzel.*

*"Kristoff? Answer me, please!" Sophie begged, her heart aching as she saw how ravaged he was.*

*"Assassin!" A loud, booming male voice came out of the fog, and Kristoff's body shuddered as a bearded god, surrounded by an unearthly aura stepped into the light. "Wake up and do my bidding."*

*Sophie suddenly realized that she was an unseen observer, the god-like creature paying her no attention, and obviously not realizing she was even present.*

*That probably meant Kristoff couldn't recognize her presence either.*

*She watched, unable to do anything to help Kristoff, as the god kicked his cage, causing Kristoff to flinch. Opening the small prison with a golden key in his hand, the god yanked his captive free. "Time to earn your keep. You have your mission?"*

*Sophie watched as Kristoff untangled his body painfully. For the first time, she noticed the golden collar around his neck, and the chain hanging from the shackle that appeared to be abrading his skin. Fresh blood flowed as the god yanked on the dangling metal, causing Kristoff's neck wounds to bleed even harder, causing specks of red to land on the god's robe.*

*"I said…do you have your mission?" the god bellowed.*

*"Yes, my king. I live only to please you, Zeus."*

*Kristoff's voice was monotone and completely devoid of emotion, much like a robot.*

*"Then go. And do not return without his head," the god insisted angrily, looking down at the droplets of blood on his pristine, white robe. "See what you did? You'll pay for that when you return."*

*He waved his hand, and Kristoff disappeared.*

*Strangely, Sophie followed him, flying through space until she landed beside him as he wielded a large machete, sneaking up behind a man in the woods who appeared to be trying to seduce a woman in a rich, blue gown. She couldn't make out the mystery woman's features because the man blocked her view. Just as before, Sophie was unable to move from her observation area.*

*Glancing from Kristoff's bleeding form to the large knife he was carrying, Sophie suddenly remembered what the god had called him.*

*Assassin?*

*What did it mean?*

*Why was Kristoff even here?*

*"You've angered the gods. For this reason, you will die," Kristoff snarled as he moved behind the male figure.*

*The unknown man barely had time to turn before Kristoff lifted his blade and divested him of his head.*

*"Oh, my God. Oh, my God. Oh, my God." Sophie's stomach rolled as blood splattered everywhere.*

*The horrified screams of the female echoed in Sophie's ears, and she began screaming herself as Kristoff grabbed the rolling head from the ground by the hair, leaving the hysterical female behind, covered in her would-be lover's blood.*

*With a cold, lifeless expression, Kristoff disappeared, and once again, Sophie followed behind.*

*She stopped screaming as she arrived in the same place she'd started, the god— who was apparently Zeus—still present in the small clearing.*

*Kristoff dropped the head of the man at the god's feet.*

*Zeus had changed his blood-spotted gown, because it was startling white once again.*

*The god nodded and instantly returned Kristoff back to his cage, locking the door with his golden key after he kicked the lifeless head Kristoff had brought him into the fog. "Tell me. Was he with Olivia?"*

*"Yes, my king," Kristoff answered, his voice totally devoid of emotion.*

*Sophie was still trembling with shock, but seeing Kristoff treated worse than a domestic pet was even worse than her fear.*

*Why? Why was he here? What had he done to deserve this kind of imprisonment?*

*"You're lucky I found a purpose for you," the god grumbled. "This is how I feel about being bled upon."*

*Zeus raised his hand and shot out a bolt of lightning that connected directly with Kristoff's body, making the cage rattle as his imprisoned body seized, smoke rising from the new wounds the jolt had created as his expression contorted with agony.*

*He didn't scream, but Sophie did it for him, shrieking loudly as she watched Kristoff being tortured, being burned alive.*

*"Stop! Leave him alone! Please." She struggled to move, but her body stayed put as she watched Zeus's torment continue.*

*He hit Kristoff again and again with bolts so powerful that his entire body was almost devoid of skin.*

*"Stop. Stop. Stop." Sophie couldn't cease her horrified screams as she watched a cruelty like she'd never known rain down on Kristoff, her feeling of helplessness to stop Kristoff's torture and pain bringing tears to her eyes.*

*The god seemed to be amusing himself, and Sophie knew if she could move and get a blade into her hand, she'd lop off the god's head without one bit of remorse.*

*Zeus. Leader of the gods?*

*He was an animal, more dark and cruel than the Evils.*

*"Kristoff!!" Her scream echoed in the small clearing, but nobody could hear her, and her head started to spin as she continued to scream with anger, mortification and frustrated fury.*

"Kristoff!"

Her cry was still ringing in the air as Sophie bolted upright in bed, still shrieking from her nightmare, tears of sorrow flowing down her face.

Putting a shaky hand over her mouth, she quieted, but shuddered in the darkness.

"It was just a dream," she whispered to herself, still trembling, unable to wipe away the images of Kristoff's suffering.

Sophie scrambled out of bed, her heart still racing, somehow knowing the images she'd seen weren't just a dream. They were somehow real, and she had to see Kristoff, assure herself that he was okay.

Crossing the room, using the moonlight from the window to guide her, she stepped into the lit hallway and ran to Kristoff's sleeping chambers.

Although he didn't need much sleep, her instincts told her that he was there right now.

She pushed his door open, and let the light into the room.

There, on the bed, was her golden demigod, his muscular body sprawled on the enormous bed.

"He's okay. He's okay. He's okay," Sophie was chanting aloud with relief. Seeing Kristoff in one piece was the only thing that was going to take away her fear.

Knowing she was invading his privacy and he'd sent her away, she started to leave. She'd seen him. He looked as gloriously beautiful as he ever had. He *wasn't* in a cage, he wasn't devoid of his golden hair, and his body was muscular and perfect.

His restlessness caused Sophie to hesitate. When he groaned as though he was in pain, and then started mumbling in a low, incoherent voice, she turned and approached the bed.

Completely on instinct, she reached out and laid a gentle hand on his shoulder. The minute their bodies connected, his thoughts shot through her brain like a rocket, and she let them. What she saw was a continuation of her own nightmare.

More punishment.

More torture.

Zeus spitting on Kristoff as he disappeared from sight.

"Bastard!" Sophie rasped, angry as she realized that she had invaded Kristoff's nightmares.

Those were no unique dreams she'd experienced. They were awful images of exactly what Kristoff was experiencing right now in his nightmares.

"Kristoff," she said urgently as she shook his shoulder and climbed into his bed. "Wake up. You're having a bad dream."

How did one wake a Sentinel demon king who was also a demigod?

She didn't get much time to ponder that question.

*Wham!*

Sophie found herself flat on her back before she realized they obviously awoke the same way a human did. Kristoff had come awake abruptly, flipping her over defensively to defend himself.

"Sophie?" he said in a dangerously displeased voice.

Looking up at him in the dim light, she babbled, "I'm sorry. You were having a nightmare, and I had it, too. I had to make sure you were okay, and I wanted you to wake up so you didn't see those things anymore."

"I saw them for thousands of years," Kristoff replied as he lifted himself off her body. "I knew you were there in the shadows. I sensed it. But I couldn't stop the dream. Now you know who and what I am," he snarled angrily. "I was an assassin for the gods, their pet killer dog for the times they didn't want to take the blame for murdering someone. Or when they just didn't want to be bothered to do the deed themselves."

"Oh, God." Sophie felt the bile rise up in her throat. "That really happened? How?"

Kristoff ran an impatient hand through his hair. "It doesn't matter. Now you understand why I don't want you to be bonded to a Sentinel like me. I've murdered thousands without remorse, a killer for anyone who displeased the gods."

Sophie knew there was more to his story, but her heart ached for what he'd been through. "You were forced."

"I agreed to do it," he answered flatly.

She stopped to consider his statement before venturing, "They tricked you."

The bedroom was silent for a moment before he answered. "I agreed," he repeated through his clenched jaw, his voice desolate. "Leave me, Sophie. Thank you for waking me, but as you can see, I'm fine."

He wasn't fine, and if he sent her away again…

*Thump!*

She landed on her bed once more, courtesy of Kristoff's demigod transport service.

"Damn him!" Sophie cursed and slammed her fist on the bed.

Flopping back onto the pillows, frustration permeating her every thought, she didn't know what to do anymore.

He wouldn't talk to her.

He wouldn't touch her.

He wouldn't let her help him.

Her body ached with need, the desire to be closer to him stronger than it ever had been. Knowing he was okay was a relief, but Sophie knew the images of Kristoff's torment would be branded forever on her brain.

Tears flowed from her eyes as her aching heart and body warred for which one was hurting the worst.

"I don't know what to do," she whispered aloud, feeling horribly alone, and more than a little confused.

The flesh between her thighs was throbbing and needy. Her nipples as hard as diamonds.

"I need him," she admitted aloud, kicking the covers off the bed as her body started to throw off so much heat it felt like she was burning alive.

In desperation, she let her hand slide down her abdomen and into her delicate panties, lifting her nightgown high as she touched herself. Her head moved from side to side as she fumbled, stroking the wet warmth that pulsated for...something more.

"Please," she gasped desperately, delving her fingers into the slick folds, hoping for relief.

Tears of despair still flowed from her eyes as she parted her legs and explored her own pussy, jolting as her finger passed over a tiny bundle of nerves, causing her sheath to clench painfully.

Rubbing harder, she felt perspiration forming on her skin, the heat coming from her body in waves.

Sobs began to escape from her lips until she felt a very large, very powerful male roll onto her bed and grasp the desperate hand between her legs as he rumbled, "Don't, Sophie. Don't cry. I'll fucking satisfy you so you don't remember the pain. You're mine to taste, mine to fuck, mine to satiate. I cut myself off from you so you didn't feel me, but that was selfish. Why didn't you tell me you needed me?"

"I tried. I asked you to fuck me," she replied angrily. "You sent me away. You do nothing but send me away. I want. I need. I crave. I feel everything you do. I know it's nothing compared to what you feel, but it hurts. Everything burns."

"It burns for me, too," he answered, his voice breaking with longing. "I just can't reconcile myself with making you settle for a filthy murderer."

"Don't say that! Don't ever say that again," Sophie snapped. "You're my mate. Nobody talks shit about my man. Not even you. What happened isn't your fault, and even if I have to wrestle with you to do it, I'm going to make your pain go away. I'm tired of trying to hide my emotions, pretend like I don't care."

"Dammit, I fucking care, too," he roared. "Too damn much, which is why I didn't want you stuck with a man who is only fit to lead a fighting force. But I'm fucking sick of always following the rules, trying to do what's right. I want to be a greedy bastard who takes exactly what he wants for once. And that would be you."

Sophie sighed as she watched his eyes turn to amber fire, and as she let herself gauge his emotions, she felt nothing except his carnal, raw, uninhibited desire. "No more holding back?"

"None. You had your chance to run, my precious mate. Your chance to escape is over. You will be mine. I will see my mark on you. I will claim you so damn hard it might be painful."

"Thank God," she whispered fervently. "I need you so much."

To her surprise, he lifted her hand carefully and licked her fingers, seeming to savor every bit of her essence as he sucked and tongued the damp fingers that had been fingering her own pussy, indulging in her taste like it was his favorite treat.

Seeing a man as strong and powerful as Kristoff licking her juices from her fingers was smoking hot, and her body reacted as she watched him, mesmerized.

"W-why? Why did you decide to come to me now?" she stammered. Now that her anger was turning into furious need, she was slightly embarrassed by being caught touching herself. It might be acceptable in today's world, but sex wasn't something even hinted or spoken about a few hundred years ago—not by females anyway.

Moving to her side, he kissed away the trail of tears from her face like her scars didn't even exist. "I can't bear your pain, and I can't block myself from you anymore. Your hunger is too strong, and it haunts me now that I can feel it. I can't stand the fact that you're unhappy, and I fucking hate it that you feel alone. I feel the emptiness, too, and I can't deny either one of us any longer. I'm here now, Sophie. Let me."

Sizzling heat ignited between her thighs, and she felt adrenaline shoot through her body. She knew what he was asking. "You want to fuck me now?"

"I've always wanted that," he grumbled, his voice hoarse with passion. "But now that your need has grown so strong, I can't ignore it."

"What about yours?"

"Your desire is more important than my own. It's the way it is between mates."

Sophie wanted to please him, too. His pain was partly hers now. His walls were starting to tumble, and her stubborn king was laying himself bare to her now.

No more fighting.

No more struggle.

No more misunderstandings.

"I would have kept fighting for you to fuck me," she whispered loud enough for him to hear.

"I would have given in," Kristoff admitted earnestly. "I've never really coveted one thing in my long existence, but you belong to me."

"I want to please you. Badly." Images of licking every inch of his muscular body and climbing him like a rock wall flitted across her mind, making her tremble. "But there's one thing you need to know. Can you turn on the light?"

He immediately used his powers to illuminate the room by turning on the lamp at the bedside. "I already know you've never been with a man, and it makes my cock so hard that I can hardly fucking breathe," he told her hoarsely. "I know I'll be the first, and I can't stand the thought of not being the last."

"That's not what I meant." Sophie rolled out of bed before she lost her courage. Standing right beside his reclining figure, she raised her arms and pulled the nightgown over her head and dropped it onto the floor. "I want you to really see me. My scars aren't just confined to areas you can see when I'm dressed."

She cringed as his fierce, flame-filled eyes took in every inch of her body, from the claw marks on her breasts, to the ones that marked her hips. Her entire body was as ugly and horrific as her face.

Turning around so he could see her demon-marked back, which was full of more proof of the Evils' torture, she slowly rotated to put her front side in his vision again, holding her breath for the look that was bound to happen—the expression of horror on his face as he saw *all* of her scars.

"Beautiful," Kristoff rasped, his voice low with unhidden carnal desire.

He reached out and grasped her fragile panties and ripped them from her body savagely without causing her a single bit of pain. "Yes," he hissed as his gaze centered on her pussy. "You're beautiful everywhere. I need to taste you."

"Kristoff, I'm starting to think you're blind." His covetous look was startling, and her whole body was one big mass of need. "Can't you even *see* my scars?"

"Come to me," he demanded, holding out his hand.

His tone was not one to be ignored. She took his hand and let him pull her onto the bed. Raising himself on his elbow, he ran rough hands over the various marks on her body, looking more turned on than disgusted.

"I do see them, and I'm angry with myself for not being there to protect you. My rage at not being able to kill Goran for you burns in my soul." He bent and ran his tongue over the mark at the side of her breast. "They're a testament of your character, your courage, and your will to survive. To me, they make you sexy. They make you the person you are—my *radiant*. You're light to my darkness, Sophie. Nothing about you will ever be unattractive. Never!"

Sophie sighed, a sound of relief and an end to her fears that Kristoff would ever see her as ugly. "I was afraid. When you rejected me, I thought you didn't want me."

He frowned, his expression annoyed. "Those are your thoughts when I'm trying to save you from me?"

She nodded slowly. "They're my insecurities."

"They will leave you," Kristoff commanded.

Sophie smiled at him, amused because he thought he could just demand her negative emotions away. But maybe, in some ways, he could. She was convinced that in his eyes, he'd never see anything that he didn't like when he looked at her naked.

As his hands became more demanding, his fingers sliding over her sensitive nipples, she moaned and closed her eyes. "They're gone," she assured him as she wrapped her arms around his neck. "Can you fuck me now?" Her body was clamoring for more. More. More.

"But you're an innocent, and now you know who and what I was—"

She quickly pressed a finger to his lips. "Don't. It's who you were, and maybe you don't want to share everything with me yet, but I want who you are now."

He quirked a surprised brow at her. "And that would be?"

"The man my body craves and my soul needs. Please, Kristoff. Teach me the thing I've never known. I'm ready to beg if I have to."

"My mate will never have to beg. My mind will never be closed to you. I can't fight this anymore," he said with a husky groan vibrating in his voice. "You taste like nectar from the gods, and I want my head between your legs, my mouth all over you until you scream out in an orgasm that will take your breath away," he told her with a carnal growl as he rolled on top of her and pinned her hands over her head. "Then I want to bury myself inside you until we're so intertwined that we can feel each other's release. This won't be the gentle claiming you deserve. It's going to be a desperate ride to pleasure.

Are you ready for that? Because I can't hold myself back. Our need is too raw."

Sophie's breath caught in her throat, and she couldn't speak as his eyes flashed to a darker amber, his expression feral and tormented.

Ready for it? Hell, she'd enjoy every second of it. "I'm not a fragile flower, Kristoff," she reminded him when she could find her voice. "You've seen the scars, the evidence."

"Nobody will ever hurt you again," he answered furiously. "I fucking swear it right now. You're mine to protect."

The more his walls crumbled, the more he was beginning to sound like a caveman, and that turned her on more than she wanted to admit. "I'm more than ready," she admitted, her hunger for him so strong that she could barely get the words out.

"Thank fuck!" Leaning down, he crushed his mouth to hers, his grasp still holding her wrists, his desperate, rough embrace claiming her.

She was breathing hard when he finally released her mouth and started to devour the sensitive skin at the side of her neck. "Mine!" he insisted in a possessive tone.

Sophie didn't argue. In the depths of her soul, she'd always known she was his. The miraculous part was that *he* was *hers*, too, and she was going to enjoy every moment of being this intimate with her mate. She allowed her body to sink into a delicious pleasure like she'd never experienced, her need to be bonded so fierce that a sharp, ferocious pain squeezed her core.

For the first time in her life, she felt truly alive, every nerve in her body sparking, and she was going to enjoy every moment of her awakening.

# Chapter Twelve

Kristoff hated himself for every harsh word he'd said to Sophie. Like a selfish prick, he'd closed himself off and hadn't been feeling her sorrow, frustration and pain.

Now that he was experiencing her need, it had him in a frenzy, frantic to soothe every ache she had. His nature and soul *demanded* it. He was slipping closer and closer to the edge of reason with every breath he took, the scent of his mate making him nearly insane.

If he could have picked one person on Earth himself to be his mate, Sophie would have been that woman. She had been worth waiting for, and his wait was fucking over. *Done.* She'd penetrated every defense he had, and he didn't care if she could see him raw and vulnerable. For her, he'd bare himself. Miraculously, he was learning to trust, and Sophie was worth risking everything to have.

His body shuddered as she whimpered when he put his mouth to her puckered nipple and teased it with his tongue. Her pleasure was his, and he'd satisfy her if it killed him.

*Mine. Mine. She was always supposed to be mine.*

And he *wanted* to claim her. Not only did she make his cock so hard it was painful, but he loved her softness, her curiosity, and her heart. Even after spending so many years with the Evils enduring their torment, Sophie still exuded an innocence that made him completely insane.

Her first concern had been for him when she'd shared his nightmares, and the fact that she cared about him felt like a blazing hot knife had stabbed him in the chest. He couldn't remember the last time that somebody had even given a shit about how he was doing other than Athena.

He was King. He was supposed to have all of the answers. But Sophie hadn't come to him for answers. She'd been checking to see if *he* was okay.

That tender action had nearly torn him apart. He'd sent her away instinctively, a last ditch effort to save her from a Sentinel who wasn't worthy, but her hurt and frustration had filtered through his crumbling mental barrier. It was a call he couldn't and wouldn't ignore.

"Kristoff, yes. Yes. Please," she cried out, her tone desperate.

His need to soothe her was so acute that he moved down her belly, tonguing every one of her scars. Those puckered marks angered him in a way that was hard to explain. Although they were a testament to her character, it killed him that he hadn't been there to protect his mate.

The burning need to see Goran dead was never going to leave him, but being able to satisfy his mate would help.

Never again would he let anybody hurt her. He'd have to be gone before that happened, and he had no plans of getting dead.

*Not when I have this. Not while I have her.*

Parting her thighs none-too-gently, he did what he'd wanted to do from the moment he'd seen Sophie. He didn't waste any time with teasing her toward climax. She needed satisfaction now, and Kristoff was determined to give her exactly what she needed.

Sophie closed her eyes as the feel of Kristoff's wicked tongue delving between her folds and licking over her clit nearly sent her flying off the bed. He used his entire mouth to devour her, and the pleasure was so intense that she couldn't stop herself from screaming.

"Oh, God! Yes! More!" She grasped his head, hanging onto him tightly. The pleasure was so intense that she tried to roll away from him.

"Mine. Mine to please," he growled in an animalistic tone. "Denied too long. You will not move."

Sophie felt herself placed onto her back again, and her hands flew over her head. Her thighs parted wide and stayed there. Her body was basically spread out and at Kristoff's mercy, her wrists and legs bound by his magic. As she strained against the invisible bonds, they held fast.

Not being able to move was erotic, knowing he was so crazed that he wasn't going to let her escape.

Kristoff returned to giving her what she needed, just the same way that he did everything: laser focused, powerfully, and with so much intensity that Sophie was gasping for breath.

She still fought the intense pleasure, but she couldn't move away, couldn't do anything but pull against his bonds, her entire body throbbing, her pussy quivering.

She thrashed on the bed as much as she could manage to move as his tongue laved her clit like it belonged to him, claimed her pussy as though it was his to pleasure. His dominance pushed Sophie's desire to fever pitch, and she panted as he flicked the tiny bundle of nerves over and over again.

"Feels. Too. Good. I can't take anymore. I can't." Sophie could barely choke out the words as she moaned incoherently.

*You'll come for me so hard that you'll forget all the pain.*

His voice was controlling, demanding, and hot as hell in Sophie's mind. She could feel his need to dominate and knew she couldn't get away. It was what he needed. And God help her, she needed it, too. Being open and submissive to Kristoff fulfilled some elemental need to be his, and the eroticism of letting him do what he willed was setting her on fire.

As he slipped a finger into her slick channel, something in her belly started to burn. When he added another, stretching her muscles as he pumped slowly in and out with his fingers as he continued to destroy her with his wicked tongue on her clit, Sophie felt the fire in her stomach begin to spread. Almost immediately, the flames went straight to her core.

"Kristoff. I can't. I can't." She wasn't sure what she was fighting, but the strength of what seemed to be overtaking her body was so forceful that it scared her.

*Come for me. I'll be here.*

The sound of his husky, demanding voice in her head tipped her over the edge. There was nothing wrong, nothing bad about to happen, even though she was beginning to burn so hot, her heart beating so fast, that she felt like she was going to die.

Trusting Kristoff completely, she let every sensation overwhelm her. The motion of his fingers matched his teasing tongue, and she let herself spiral out of control.

When her climax gripped her, she screamed, her back arching up, and her nails digging into her palms.

"Oh, God. Kristoff!" The muscles of her sheath clenched down on Kristoff's fingers over and over and she physically shook when the volatile orgasm reached its peak.

She struggled for breath as she began to spin down again, hearing Kristoff lapping eagerly at the juices she'd expelled as she'd been rocked by her first orgasm.

She sighed as the bonds holding her released, and he slid up her body and nuzzled her neck. "Better now?" he asked hoarsely.

The feel of his whiskered jaw against her sensitive skin felt sinfully erotic. "Better," she agreed. "Can I do the same thing to you now?" She wanted to taste him the same way he'd done to her. In fact, she craved it.

"I'd never survive it," he answered unhappily, his voice muffled against her neck. "If you took my cock between those beautiful lips of yours, I'd lose my mind."

She smiled and speared her hands through his hair, which was now damp with sweat. His solemn answer actually delighted her, even though she hated seeing him suffering. Knowing he wanted her *just that much* was heady for her.

Wriggling beneath him, she encouraged, "Fuck me, then. Please." She could feel his enormous, rock-hard cock between their bodies, and she needed him. "I still need you. I need to feel you."

"I'm not sure I'll survive that either, but I can't stop myself," Kristoff growled between gritted teeth. "It might hurt. You're so damn tight. I warned you that this would be a rough ride."

"I don't care," she mumbled, her sheath aching to take him in. "Now, Kristoff. Do it now."

She wasn't certain if she was feeling the pain of his need or hers, but it didn't matter. Knowing Kristoff needed relief was the only thing she could think about, her only focus.

He filled her with one swift thrust of his hips, groaning as he buried his cock deeply inside her. "Jesus, Sophie. You're slick, but so damn tight. Do you know how good it feels to be the only man who has had you like this? The only man that ever will?"

Taking a moment to catch her breath from the momentary pain of having Kristoff's cock embedded to the root inside her, it took her a minute to answer. "No. I only know how it feels to have you there. It fills the emptiness."

"You'll never be without me again," he vowed furiously. "If I have my way, you'll never be empty."

Sophie was pretty sure he'd get his way, because she could feel that he was experiencing the same fleeing of the loneliness they'd both experienced their entire lives.

After the initial shock of accepting him and the intense stretching of her muscles, his cock felt incredible. He was big and powerful, and her euphoria filled all of her senses.

Instinctively, she wrapped her legs around his hips, pulling him tighter against her as he began to move.

"Can't. Go. Slow." His voice was low and raspy.

"Don't," she begged. "Fuck me like you mean it."

For just a little while, she wanted to feel like his *radiant*, the woman he wanted above all others.

"I do mean it," he answered as he slammed into her over and over again. "You're all I want, Sophie. Everything I've ever needed."

She held onto him tightly as his hands went under her ass and guided her. As he pummeled into her, he pulled her up, as though he needed her to take every inch of him inside her with every stroke of his cock.

"Mine!" he snarled as he moved faster and faster. "Tell me you're mine, Sophie. Say it out loud before I lose my fucking mind."

"I'll always be yours, Kristoff." She gave him what he needed willingly. The words left her without thinking, probably because she knew them to be true. In some small part of her soul, she'd always been his, and always would be.

Perspiration formed on their bodies as they struggled to satisfy the unbearable carnal desire that was now in control.

Sophie babbled incoherently as her senses took over. "Yes. Fuck me, Kristoff. Claim me."

"Mine!" he growled. "Always mine."

Just as Sophie felt that fire beginning to shoot between her thighs and the first waves of her climax start to pulsate through her body, Kristoff grasped her hands from around his neck and pinned them over her head. "Never giving you up," he vowed, his eyes flashing a brilliant amber as he lowered his head and started to kiss her with a desperation that took her breath away.

She moaned against his lips as her sheath clamped down on his cock, squeezing it with every frenzied thrust of his hips.

When he lifted his mouth, he groaned. "Jesus, Sophie. Nothing's ever felt this damn good."

As she neared her peak, she arched her back in tortured pleasure, her sensitive nipples abrading against his chest. "Yes. Oh, yes," she hissed, having caught onto his rhythm and moving her hips up to meet his, driving him deeper inside her.

His brilliant gaze met hers, and she watched his tormented pleasure/pain expression as she milked him of his own release. He spilled himself deep inside her womb with a satisfied groan that filled Sophie with an animalistic satisfaction.

They came down together, Kristoff lowering his forehead to hers as they both panted for air, their bodies overheated and slick with sweat.

When she finally caught her breath, she pulled her wrists loose from his grip and wrapped her arms around him. "I didn't know it could be like that."

He rolled to her side to keep her from having to take his weight. Not that she would have minded. The minute he disconnected their bodies, Sophie instantly felt the loss.

"It's not always like that," Kristoff told her, swiping the damp strands of hair from her face. "Believe me."

Sophie didn't think she wanted to know how many women he'd had in the past. Her own possessive instincts were starting to strengthen, and the last thing she wanted was to picture her mate with another woman.

"No need to be jealous," Kristoff said, amused. He stroked her cheek with his fingertip as he admitted, "Other than Talia's mother, there hasn't been anyone for thousands of years. Before I became the Sentinel king."

"Before that?" she asked bluntly.

"Not that many, really. And I was only a young man." He hesitated before adding, "Nothing in the human realm could have ever prepared me for this. For you."

He pulled her body over his, and Sophie sighed as she rested her head on his chest, lulled by the solid beat of his heart.

She wanted to ask him about their dreams. There were so many things she didn't understand about his past.

"Tomorrow," Kristoff said as though he'd read her mind, which he probably had. "Right now, let me take care of you like I always should have done."

He lifted her easily and took her into the shower. He washed her sated body slowly, carefully. It occurred to Sophie that he could have easily just cleaned them with his powers, but he seemed to want to touch her, to be close to her.

After drying her and combing out her wet hair, he swept her up into his arms and carried her back to his bed.

"You sleep with me, Sophie," he informed her bossily, but with a touch of vulnerability in his tone.

As she cuddled against him, she sighed when he spooned their naked bodies together. "Always. I want to stay with you forever." Her brain had no filter anymore. Kristoff had laid her bare, and she was speaking from her heart.

He didn't answer, but she could hear him expel the air he'd been holding in his lungs that sounded an awful lot like a *whooshed* breath of relief.

She fell asleep in Kristoff's warm, covetous embrace, sleeping an exhausted slumber where she felt safe for the very first time in her life.

# Chapter Thirteen

"So what I saw in my dreams last night was real?" Sophie asked carefully the next morning as she ate from the mountain of food Kristoff had created on her breakfast plate. At the rate she was going with food, she'd be bursting out of her jeans within another couple of days.

He nodded sharply, giving her a warning glance across the small table in the foyer. Since Athena had never created a kitchen in this home, it was their usual gathering place for meals. Sophie knew from his closed expression that he didn't want to talk about their shared dreams. But she was determined to get her answers.

"Tell me," she encouraged quietly.

"What is there to really tell?" he retorted. "Everything you saw is true. I was the gods' assassin. It was my job for centuries."

Her stomach beginning to churn, Sophie laid down her fork and reached for her coffee. "Zeus caged you that way for that long? Why?"

"Because he was a narcissistic pig," Kristoff answered angrily. "Everything revolved around him in his world." He took a deep breath and continued, "I never fit into the human world. My human mother shunned me, and I was raised by a decent couple who fed me and took care of me—until they realized I had powers I couldn't control. It scared them, so they turned their back on me, too. I can't really blame them. In the human world, I was a freak, and I had no idea how to control the powers of a god."

"Your father never contacted you?" Sophie's heart ached for a confused young man who didn't know what to do with the powers he'd gained from a god.

"No. I had to track him when I knew I couldn't stay in the human world any longer without help."

"Did he help you?"

Kristoff let out a bark of laughter that didn't contain any hint of humor. "If you can call it that. Once I found him, he promised me a place in the world of the gods. He said if I'd take an open position, he'd teach me how to use my powers." He paused before continuing, "I agreed, but I didn't know the open position was as the assassin for the gods. I was young enough and lost enough to do anything to figure out exactly who and what I was."

"Oh, God. Please don't tell me Zeus was your father." Sophie felt her breakfast rolling around in her belly. She already knew what Kristoff's answer would be.

"He was. And I wasn't an offspring he wanted to claim. I was only a demigod, a bastard of very little importance, a son to scorn."

"Bastard!" Sophie cursed, wishing Zeus to Hades for what he'd done to Kristoff.

A small smile formed on Kristoff's sensual lips. "It was mostly my fault. Never trust a god. I agreed to his proposal hoping for a father, and I ended up with the cruelest jailer imaginable. He did show me how to use my powers, but only for evil. Eventually, he bent me completely to his will. He might have been an asshole, but he was powerful."

"It wasn't your fault. You didn't have any choice," Sophie defended staunchly.

Kristoff shrugged. "I refused to kill for him at first, but I eventually succumbed to his torture. I was still young, and my will wasn't very strong. In time, I was forced to do his bidding. He was the king of the gods, and I was his son. There was no way to fight it."

"He was a monster," Sophie answered furiously. "I saw how he treated you, how you were conditioned. Did you ever feel remorse?"

"In the beginning. But eventually I lost all of my free will. I didn't think. I simply reacted to commands."

"I don't understand why you blame yourself for your past."

He shrugged. "I chose my fate. I went to him."

"You wanted a father," Sophie protested loudly. "You wanted to understand who you were and how to control your power. Nobody can blame you for that. How did you finally break his control?"

"Once Athena became aware of my existence and rescued me, I changed. I felt remorse. I felt responsible for every person I ever killed, even if most of them weren't very nice people. I have the blood of a thousand on my hands, Sophie."

"So you think you deserve to be punished for the rest of your existence?" She understood very well how it felt to be helpless, to be forced to do things she didn't want to do.

He pinned her with a glacial stare. "Don't I? I was a killer. It was my only purpose for centuries."

"No. You don't," Sophie answered angrily. "Zeus deserves to be spending eternity in Hades for what he did, but you don't need to spend the rest of your life paying for being young and confused. I'm just glad Athena finally pulled you out of that horrific cage." Taking an audible breath, her chest rising and falling with frustration, Sophie suddenly realized something that hadn't been said. "Athena is your sister."

"Half-sister," Kristoff corrected. "I owe her my sanity and my life. When her father accidentally let it slip that he had his own private assassin and that I was related to her, she found me. It took me years to trust her, and even longer to like her. By the time she offered to make me a Sentinel king, I was ready to take on something that actually meant something, to be someone who was fighting for humanity instead of executing all of the people who had angered the gods."

"You've paid your dues, done your penance for something that really wasn't your fault," Sophie told him gently.

"How do you ever pay enough for slaying a thousand people?" Kristoff asked with a frown. "I can't undo what I was."

"Do you think I don't know how you feel?" Sophie rasped. "Do you think I don't feel remorse for every woman that died in the demon realm? Do you think I don't feel like I'm drowning in guilt because I lived while so many women died over the centuries I was there?" She took a deep breath before continuing to let her emotions go. "I feel it *here* every day." She put a hand over her heart. "*I* lived and *they* didn't. Eventually, I had to block out that pain or give the Evils more ammunition to torture me with. You did exactly the same thing. I feel it, Kristoff. I lived it." She rose with a tormented sob.

Faster than lightning, Kristoff caught her in his arms. "Don't! Your situation is different. You didn't kill those women."

"It's not different. I could have fought for them, but I didn't. At first, I didn't understand. When I finally figured out they were dead, I didn't know how to protect them. I knew it was futile. There was nothing I could do. But I still can't forget them." Burying her face against his shoulder, the tears and sobs kept coming.

He stroked a comforting hand over her hair. "You're tormenting yourself for no reason. Don't."

"I'll lay it to rest when you do," she told him adamantly. "When we can both find peace with what happened to us, then I'll stop hating myself for being the only woman who lived."

"Sweetheart, I can't— "

"You can," Sophie interrupted. "You can finally admit that you didn't have the power back then to fight your father. That he was the murderer, not you. You had no control back then. He did."

"If I try to remember that, will you stop crying?" Kristoff asked huskily.

Sophie let out a snort that was part laughter and partly a sob. "Yes."

"Then I will try. I can't bear to see you blame yourself for something that was way beyond your control."

"Ditto," she answered, using the new slang word she'd seen in a movie she'd watched just a few days ago.

Kristoff let out a bark of laughter that contained humor this time. "You're so prepared to fight for me?"

Sophie pulled back and stared up at him. "Of course. I'm your *radiant*. I'll always fight for you."

Strangely, knowing Kristoff was her destined partner didn't faze her a bit anymore. Since he'd touched her, claimed her, she knew things were exactly the way they were supposed to be. Well...if he wasn't so damn stubborn about the *radiant* thing.

His face became solemn. "You don't deserve to be stuck with a Sentinel like me. You should have someone who makes you happy."

"You made me happy last night?"

He quirked his brow. "By sharing my nightmares with you?"

Sophie batted at his shoulder playfully. "You know that wasn't what I meant. It was something I'll never forget."

He stroked a lock of hair from her face. "Believe me, I'll never forget it either. But my need to make you belong to me forever is growing stronger. I either have to find a way to break us apart, or you're going to end up mine forever. Truthfully, I will end up making you mine. I can't let you go."

It was that moment of tenderness, and his concern for her that really broke Sophie. "You can't force me. Athena explained how things work."

"No. No, I can't," he rasped.

"What if I don't want you to control it anymore? What if I wanted to be your mate forever, my stubborn Sentinel king?"

Her heart accelerated as she stared at him, their eyes locking and holding. In that moment, Sophie could feel everything he was experiencing. The intense longing almost brought her to her knees.

"What are you saying?" Kristoff asked gruffly, need and desire turning his blue-eyed stare bright amber.

He looked hopeful, an expression Sophie had never seen in his grim countenance before. "I'm saying that maybe I want to be your mate. Maybe we really are perfect for each other. Maybe the fates got it right." She took his hand and placed it over her heart. "I feel it here, Kristoff, and it feels good. Scary, but like a miracle at the same time. I've never had somebody who was mine. I've always been alone. Sharing your thoughts, being that close to a man is overwhelming, but not in a bad way."

He grabbed her by the shoulders, his expression feral and intense. "You have no idea how much I crave you. I want to see you wearing my mark, and I feel like I'll never recover from the pain if I can't join us together and have you bonded to me as my mate. But I don't want you to regret it someday. My responsibilities as the Sentinel king are heavy at times. I can be a major asshole."

His capitulation made Sophie's heart sing. "Maybe I like assholes, and I'd never let you get too out of line," she ventured hesitantly, knowing she wanted to share the burdens that Kristoff refused to reveal to anyone. "I know what it's like to be alone."

A low growl reverberated through the air. "You're mine. You're not alone, and you'll never be alone again. It's my job as your mate to take care of you in every way, a responsibility I'd be happy and humbled to have."

*Longing.*

All she felt was a desperate desire so intense that Sophie could hardly breathe. Lifting a hand to stroke his jaw, she whispered, "Then join us. I'll take my duties to make you happy seriously, too. I feel some of your pain, and it's tearing us both apart."

They were in Kristoff's bedroom as fast as Sophie could blink. "You make me happy just by breathing, just by being with me," he answered huskily.

"I can do much better than that," she said as she looked up at the man who had stolen her heart. He'd been alone for too long. And she was going to make damn sure he always knew that he had a mate at his back.

"Promise me that you won't regret this, love," he demanded gruffly. "Promise that you won't one day hate being mated to a murderer."

Sophie sighed as she looked at her would-be partner for life. His expression was serious and drawn, as though he expected her to re-think her decision. "I won't regret it. You're the only man I've been with, and the only one I've ever wanted. I know in my heart that will never change."

He stroked a gentle finger over her cheek. "How does an asshole like me get lucky enough to be given a woman like you? I still don't understand this."

Kristoff's humble comment hit Sophie straight in the heart. "Because you deserve to be happy. Someday I'll make you believe that," she answered honestly.

"One day you'll wake up and realize you were wrong," he warned her.

"One day you'll wake up and realize I'm not beautiful," she teased him back.

"Don't say that," he commanded. "There will never be a day when I don't want you just as much as I do right now. You're everything to me now, Sophie. You're my entire life. There will never be a morning when I don't wake up fucking grateful you were willing to have me."

Her heart skipped a beat, and her core clenched with a need so strong she could barely answer. "I hope not."

"*Will* you have me then, sweet Sophie? Will you share your soul with me, faults and all?" He sounded worried, like he was afraid she'd change her mind.

She nodded instantly. "Yes." How could a woman ever turn down Kristoff? He thought they were so different, but really, they were so much alike.

They'd both been ruled by their insecurities and their past, but it was time for all of that to stop.

She knew deep down in her soul that she'd never be happy unless she became his *radiant* and was bonded to him. Her entire being was clamoring to be joined with this lonely Sentinel king who'd been waiting eons for his *radiant*. In truth, maybe she'd been waiting for him for him, too, even though she hadn't really known it while she was imprisoned in the demon realm. She'd survived, and the only reason she was still here was because she had a purpose here on Earth right now.

Together, they would heal each other. Sophie could sense it. But she also knew that time was running out. As well as Kristoff hid his pain, it was there, and it was intense.

*I won't lose him just because of my fears or his unwarranted sense of guilt.*

Athena had made it clear that Kristoff could only bear so much, and Sophie didn't want him to hurt anymore.

Kristoff didn't give her a chance to utter another word.

The minute her answer had left her lips, he swooped down and claimed her mouth, letting her know in no uncertain terms that he was way beyond talking anymore.

Her fate was sealed, and Sophie couldn't dredge up a single ounce of remorse.

# Chapter Fourteen

Sophie was so lost in Kristoff's volatile embrace that she hardly noticed when their clothing disappeared. If it hadn't been for the sudden flash of heat when their bare bodies suddenly merged, and the sensual sensation of skin against skin, she would have been oblivious to everything. His carnal taking of her mouth as he demanded her submission nearly scrambled her brain.

His powerful arm wrapped around her waist, pulling her flush against him while he used his other hand to spear into her hair and position her mouth exactly where he wanted it. His tongue penetrated deeper into the cavern, sweeping desperately, like he needed to own every inch of her.

Finally, he tore his mouth from hers as though it was painful for him to separate them, and he forcefully uttered words in what sounded like an ancient language in a deep voice that sent shivers down her spine. His eyes deepened to a beautiful blue color she'd never seen before, and it was breathtaking to watch as they changed to a shade so dark that they were almost black rather than a deep navy blue.

For an instant, Sophie was perplexed. She knew he'd just spoken the vow to join them as mates, but it wasn't happening the way Athena had explained it. No shackles appeared, and suddenly, the same words came flowing from her lips, even though she didn't have a clue what she was saying.

"I don't understand," she whispered, still panting from Kristoff's embrace.

"Follow your instincts. The actions will come to you just like they're being revealed to me. Our joining is different. Just go with it," Kristoff urged her. "Put your legs around my waist."

Obviously, the king's mating was going to be different, and Sophie opened her mind to him. His emotions hit her full force, telling her that he'd completely merged his thoughts and emotions with hers. Pain racked her body, but she lifted her arms up as her intuition led her to do, and they both looked up as silken ties floated down from the ceiling.

Kristoff moved forward, and her back connected with the wall as the ties lashed around her wrists. She gripped them, her fingers wrapping around the soft, velvety surface of the dangling ropes as her body continued to shake from the force of the red-hot burning sensation she was experiencing.

"It hurts," she whimpered, feeling like a hot branding iron was marking her everywhere.

"Fuck!" Kristoff rasped. "You're feeling me."

Sophie looked down at him with a desire so carnal and possessive that she wanted to crawl inside Kristoff and never leave. "I need you, Kristoff. I need you."

"Mine! You're going to be mine," he growled, his dark eyes locking with Sophie's in a gaze so intense it was startling.

His mouth clamped onto one of her hard nipples, making Sophie moan helplessly as he brought both his big hands up and claimed her breasts. His grip was rough, but she welcomed it.

She needed to feel him.

She needed him to claim her just like this.

"Yes!" she squealed as his hand closed over her breasts with a rough caress that satisfied her feral need. "More!" With her arms stretched over her head, and her legs locked around Kristoff's hips, she was at his mercy, something that seemed to satisfy his caveman need to have her unable to get away from him.

His mouth moved back and forth from one hardened peak to the other, his hands touching, claiming every inch of her sensitive breasts.

Sophie longed to have her hands on him, but she knew that this was the way it was supposed to be. The intense burn she was experiencing was everything Kristoff had felt for the last few weeks. How he'd endured it she wasn't certain.

"My beautiful mate," he said in a husky voice as he lifted his head.

Her core clenched painfully as the timbre of his voice vibrated through her, the emptiness of not yet having him inside her nearly killing her. "Fuck me, Kristoff. Hard. I need it all. Give me everything you're feeling because I'm feeling it, too," she told him breathlessly.

She was right with him, experiencing everything he was with their minds merged.

He moved his hands, running them slowly down her back, his knuckles scraping the wall as he cupped her ass and squeezed.

Helplessly, she rubbed her soaked pussy against him, gripping him harder with her legs as she rubbed against his hard, six-pack abs.

"Stop!" Kristoff demanded. "I don't want to hurt you."

"I don't care," she argued fiercely, grinding against him again, rotating her hips to feel his hard muscles against her core, trying to get the stimulation she wanted. "Fuck me. I want it hard. I want it real."

"Be careful what you wish for, love," he answered back gruffly. "I'm. Not. In. Control."

The four measured words fueled Sophie's desire for Kristoff to finally lose it.

When she humped against him again, her pussy so wet that she left his stomach damp, she got exactly what she wanted.

"You're ready," he snarled. "I don't want to hurt you, but I can't bear the thought that you're feeling what I'm feeling."

She met his gaze with a fiery look of her own. "I do. I feel like I'm on fire."

"Then we burn together," he growled as he lifted her, positioned himself, then buried his rock-hard cock inside her with one swift thrust.

Sophie gasped and tightened her grip on the silken cords, her nails biting into the skin of her palms. "Oh, God. Yes. More. More. Please don't hold back. I'm not going to break. I need this. I need you." She was willing to beg to have him join them hot, hard and with so much intensity that they nearly burnt each other up.

He gripped her ass tightly, not really holding her up because her bindings supported her. It was more a gesture of possessiveness, and a way to enter her more deeply as he began to pound into her with an abandon that matched Sophie's needs. He was rough, led by his basic instincts to claim her completely.

She moaned with every pump and grind of his hips as he pummeled into her, seeming to drive deeper with every single stroke.

Suddenly, she was lost.

Lost to the punishing rhythm.

Lost in the erotic, carnal sensation as she heard his grunt of satisfaction.

Lost as their bodies slapped together erotically.

Lost in the pounding intensity of her impending climax.

"Please," she begged, needing something she couldn't identify.

"Mine. Mine. Finally fucking mine!" Kristoff's graveled, low, covetous voice rumbled.

"Yes," she panted, her head hitting the wall as she gave her body up to the roar of her approaching orgasm and to *him*.

Her body imploded as Kristoff's hands roamed over her, his fingers coming back slick as he encountered the place where they were joined. "So wet for me. For *me*," he grunted, slipping one of those soaked fingertips into her anus and pumping in shallow motion that matched what he was doing with his cock.

The blatantly erotic sensation of being completely taken made her climax intensify, sending her completely over the edge as she felt his teeth sink into her shoulder. The action was painful, but it was so damn carnally gratifying that it didn't matter. She was filled with a satisfaction, a euphoric high that was as exhilarating as it was frightening.

"Kristoff," she screamed, instinct demanding she mark him for her own as she continued to rock against his sweat-dampened body.

Without thinking, she lowered her head as her sheath began to clamp down on his cock. She opened her mouth, licking greedily against the spot on his shoulder where she knew she had to bite, then clamped down hard with her teeth and mouth.

"Oh, fuck! Yeah. Claim me as hard as you want to. Mark me as yours," Kristoff groaned as he let go of his bite on her shoulder and buried his face in her breasts.

Sophie *did* mark him hard, hanging onto his skin with her teeth as her channel milked Kristoff's cock, his hips continuing to pound her against the wall until he finally roared her name. "Sophie."

Her heart skittered as she heard him say her name so possessively that it moved her to tears. "I'm here, Kristoff. I'm here." Her voice was muffled against his shoulder.

She knew he needed reassurance as his orgasm peaked and he spilled his fiery release deep inside her.

Sophie moved her mouth from his shoulder and shivered as her orgasm began to spiral back down and the silken bindings released her wrists and disappeared.

Suddenly, Kristoff was Sophie's only support, but he appeared to barely notice that he'd taken her full weight as he moved over to the bed and gently laid them down, his cock still inside her as he let her sprawl over him on the mattress.

Neither one spoke, but it didn't matter. Sophie knew that Kristoff was feeling the exact same sensation of soul-deep connection that she was experiencing right now.

It felt divine.

It felt real.

And it was everything Sophie had always longed for but didn't know it.

Her aloneness was gone, and in its place was her thoughts and emotions melded with Kristoff's. A bigger piece of each of their souls had been replaced with the others, and it felt amazing.

Finally, she stirred, nuzzling the side of his neck as she said, "Well, that wasn't exactly the way Athena explained it."

Kristoff ran a gentle hand down her back. "It was different. I can only assume it's because I'm different."

"You're the king. Apparently you aren't made to be submissive to anyone," she answered as she smiled and ran her fingers through his hair. Her heart was still racing, but her soul felt at peace.

"You'll always be my weakness and my strength, Sophie. And my equal. My mate," Kristoff answered as his hand kept stroking her back, his tone not displaying anything except wonder and gratitude.

"That's good because I'm afraid I'm not made to be the silent type who follows orders without questions," she answered with a laugh. "Except maybe in bed." There, she rather liked Kristoff's dominate nature.

Kristoff rolled her under him, and Sophie was startled when she saw the wicked, lopsided grin on his face. He looked...happy. Since she hadn't seen him show much joy since they'd met, it made her heart melt.

"Does that mean you won't obey me, woman?" he boomed in a mocking voice.

She chewed her lip, enjoying his playful side. "Probably not very often," she retorted jokingly. "I just got my freedom after a couple of centuries of being stuck in the demon realm. I think I need to... explore." Her voice turned sultry as she ran her palm down his muscular chest.

Their eyes caught and held, and she marveled at the adoration she saw in his beautiful eyes, which had now returned to a startling baby blue.

"I'll cherish you forever," he uttered huskily, as though he was stating a solemn vow.

Sophie had no doubt that he would. She'd come to know Kristoff would never say anything he didn't mean. "And I'll always be grateful that you see beyond my scars," she answered, her eyes glistening with happy tears.

Hideous to most, but adored by a king. Sophie still couldn't fathom why a man as physically perfect as Kristoff wanted her so desperately. But little by little, she was learning not to question his attachment to her. Being his *radiant* made her beautiful in his eyes.

"It isn't just our bond," Kristoff told her emphatically. "It's you, sweetheart. Your heart. Your courage. Your strength in surviving and now trying to adjust to a whole new world. You're special, Sophie."

"Just like you are," she whispered gently, brushing a lock of golden hair from his forehead. "You did the same things." She covered his lips with her fingers as he started to protest. "You did, Kristoff. Everything that happened to you was out of your control. Let it go. I want to start our life together."

She held her breath, hoping he'd finally realize that none of his existence when he was held under Zeus's thumb was his fault. The thought of what he'd suffered made her time spent in the demon realm seem almost easy.

"It's hard to forget how many lives I took, and that they didn't happen in battle," he admitted harshly.

"They did," Sophie protested. "You were battling to stay alive. Please stop blaming yourself. You've spent centuries trying to make up for it, even though it wasn't your fault. Do you really think anyone could have fought the king of the gods? You've paid your dues. You were given a life you didn't ask for; a life you didn't choose. You were only a young man when you went looking for your own kind so you didn't have to feel displaced and lost. You were betrayed when you found your father. When it came time for you to make your own decisions after Athena came to take you away from Zeus's torture, you dedicated yourself to helping save humanity. Don't you deserve one thing for yourself now?"

She watched as indecision passed over his expression before his lips twitched up in a small smile again. "It seems I do. I have you."

Her heart flip-flopped as she *felt* him give in. Now that they were bonded, she was tightly in his soul and his mind, and she knew exactly what he was thinking. His reasoning was skewed, Kristoff oh-so-willing to take on the blame for what he'd done. But her arguments were affecting his thoughts, making him start to see the real truth.

She turned her head and looked at the marking on his shoulder. Touching the mark reverently, she replied, "Yes, you do have me now. And I'm not going to spend our lives letting you wallow in guilt."

Kristoff pulled back slightly and kissed the set of twin flames on Sophie's shoulder. "Mine," he rasped, his eyes starting to flash to amber as he touched the marking. "It's bigger than the ones all of the other Sentinels and their *radiants* have. I like it."

There was so much smug satisfaction in her mate's voice that she laughed. "Bigger is better?"

His grin got wider. "Always," he quipped back, knowing he'd caught Sophie with her words.

She snorted. "Are we still talking about mating marks?" She kind of doubted it since she could feel his cock harden against her belly.

"No," he admitted, his golden head swooping down to capture her lips.

Something in Sophie's belly fluttered as she wrapped her arms around his neck, savoring his intensity.

Then, as her body started clamoring for Kristoff's possession, she felt herself desensitizing, his touch getting lighter and lighter. As he lifted his head, she shouted, panicked as she seemed to be pulling away from him. "Kristoff. What's happening?"

"Sophie. Goddamn it! No. Don't you dare leave me. Fuck!" Kristoff's voice was a frantic roar as he reached out for his mate.

The king of the Sentinels ended up in bed alone. As he cursed, Sophie faded away until she disappeared, leaving him naked, alone, and one furiously angry Sentinel.

# Chapter Fifteen

"I don't give a fuck if she's probably discovering her hidden talent. I want her back, and I want her *now*."

Kristoff paced Athena and Hunter's living room, still not able to calm his rage that Sophie had disappeared. His half-sister was trying to make him see reason, but he felt nothing except the desperate need to see his mate, make certain she was safe.

"Kristoff, you know how the special mates have disappeared because they are pulled to their destiny as soon as they're mated. I'm sure she's fine. You know she is," Athena said emphatically, stepping in front of him so he'd stop pacing.

Hunter was sitting on the sofa, and he finally spoke. "What if she isn't?" he chimed in.

Athena gave her mate a dirty look.

"Well, it's bullshit," Hunter protested. "I know how Kristoff feels. How many of the special mates have actually been fine when they were pulled away after mating?" he ended morosely.

Athena frowned at him as she answered, "We don't know she *isn't* fine."

Hunter gave her a belligerent look. "We don't know that she *is*. Kat ended up lost in demon hell, Talia flashed to me, which wasn't such a bad thing, but I was kind of an asshole back then. I could have hurt her."

"Back then?" Athena said huffily.

"Say what you want, but you didn't end up in such a great place either," Hunter reminded his mate.

"Fuck!" Kristoff exploded, moving Athena out of the way so he could move again. He was restless and quite honestly horrified by imagining where his mate could be right now. "Thanks for reminding me," he growled at Hunter.

Athena propped her hands on her hips. "Just where do you expect us to look for her? You mated with her. You should have a connection to her. What's happening? Where is she?"

"I don't know. Dammit! I can't feel her!" For Kristoff, that was the scariest part of his mate's disappearance.

He'd followed her essence, able to track her only so far before he lost his communication with her. It was as if her thoughts had suddenly closed off completely.

"Where in the hell is my sister?" Zach bellowed as he popped into the room with Kat.

"She's gone. We mated and she disappeared," Kristoff admitted as he glared at Zach.

Kristoff felt himself suddenly slammed against the wall, his mate's angry brother holding him against the surface by his neck.

"You swore you'd protect her. She can't be gone. Not again," Zach said angrily.

He *had* failed Zach, and he could see the look of anguish on his face, even though his tone was furious. But he was already on the edge. He shoved Zach away, sending him flying until his Sentinel slammed into the wall on the other side of the room.

"I know you're pissed off," Kristoff told Zach angrily. "But stay the fuck off me. I just lost my mate. I don't need your shit right now."

Athena spoke up and turned to Zach. "You have no right to be angry. You lost your own mate when you bonded, and Kristoff pulled your ass out of the fire. Maybe you should remember *that*."

Kat raced to Zach's side, but she stayed silent as she made sure he wasn't injured.

"Maybe you should all get a grip." The words came from a much calmer Drew who had just appeared with Talia seconds earlier. "Is this bickering going to help Sophie?"

Kristoff shook his head, knowing his most levelheaded Sentinel was right. He needed to connect with Sophie, but he still couldn't feel her, and her silence was driving him toward madness. Being bonded, then losing his connection made him dangerously unstable.

"What happened?" Drew asked in a rational voice.

Athena quickly explained to Drew what had occurred.

Drew nodded. "Athena is right. We know Sophie is a special *radiant*. She must have a skill that could possibly be out-of-control right now." He hesitated before asking, "You really can't connect with her?"

"No," Kristoff snapped.

Zach and Kat drew closer, the look on Zach's face somber as his mate ventured, "What could her skill be? I think all of the Sentinels felt the balance snap back into place when Kristoff mated with Sophie. The release of Sophie's power was noticeable. That's why we came here. It's probably why Drew and Talia did, too."

The couple nodded their agreement.

"What need do we still have?" Athena asked, almost as if she was talking to herself.

"The prophecies didn't give us a clue," Talia observed. "I never thought about the fact that Sophie was obviously going to have a special power since her actions of bonding to Kristoff righted the Universe again. We're rock solid. I thought that would be her contribution."

Kristoff had never thought about it either, but he wished he had. He had needed Sophie, and he could sense she needed him, too. The fact that she'd disappear to go find her destiny had never fucking entered his mind.

"I need to go probe for her," Kristoff decided. "I'll search every damn dimension on Earth to see if I can make contact with her."

"It's not the dimension that's blocking her," Zach argued. "You should still be able to reach out to her. It has to be Sophie blocking you."

"She can't," Kristoff countered. "She doesn't have the power to block me, and we're bonded now. There's something else happening."

Unable to sit and try to reason anything out, Kristoff left Hunter's home, determined to search as long as he had to in order to bring his mate back to his side.

He needed her, and deep down he knew that she needed him, too.

He didn't question it.

He didn't second guess whether or not he deserved her.

He was done living a half-life.

Wherever Sophie was right now, he'd find her, and he was determined to make her happy.

*I just need the chance.*

He regretted every moment that he'd spent fighting their bond. When he should have embraced it, he'd fought like hell not to give in. Now, she belonged to him. Sophie was his to protect, his to adore, his to spoil, and he'd start just as soon as he had her by his side again.

"Kristoff?" Athena yelled as her half-brother disappeared.

He didn't hear her. The king had already gone in search of his mate.

Sophie had appeared in a place she'd never been before, dazed at first because she didn't recognize the man she was watching.

Knowledge came to her effortlessly, and she knew instantly that the dark-haired man lying in his bed was a warrior Sentinel, one who had fought the recent war against the Evils. He was still recovering, but his eyes were opening slowly. As she held her breath, afraid what he'd think of her just appearing in his home, she breathed a sigh of relief that he obviously couldn't see her.

She was like a phantom that he was unable to visualize as he looked around his empty home groggily.

*He needs his mate!*

As weird as everything was right now, Sophie didn't question the fact that she knew that this Sentinel's intended mate had been one of the women who had died at the hands of the Evils. An unbound *radiant* who had died a few decades ago.

*Bethany!*

She was one of the unfortunate women that Sophie remembered well and had befriended.

Relaxing, feeling the urgency to fall into another dimension, Sophie allowed herself to float until she reached a small space that was brilliant with light.

"Mate of Sentinel warrior, Randolph...come to me." The words left her mouth in a loud command, and her hand stretched out to grasp the bolt of light that raced toward her.

*Bethany's soul. It's been kept here all this time, and the rest of them are all here, too. They were never really gone. They were all...waiting.*

A heart-pounding happiness spurred Sophie on with her task, leaving the light-filled dimension and letting herself be taken to the woman who would be Randolph's mate.

It didn't surprise her when she appeared in a strange house, but her heart ached as she saw a woman crying at a small kitchen table, her face in her hands, her sobs so heartbreaking that Sophie could see her pain.

*Some man used her and left her. She thinks she'll never be loved.*

Sophie sensed immediately that the weeping woman's soul was so broken that it would never heal. Time after time, she'd searched for a man who would love her just the way she was. And time after time, she'd been hurt even more than the time before until she had nothing left to give. No man had ever adored her, and like Sophie herself, the female was desolate that her physical appearance was going to keep her from finding the man she dreamed of encountering.

"Not an earthly one," Sophie muttered to herself. "It's not your destiny."

This woman had been born to be a *radiant*, but she'd lacked the *radiant* energy and a target male.

Sophie realized there were other women like this, females born to replace the mates of those who had perished. They'd never be happy, never find the man they longed for because they were fated to be something...more. They were meant to be with a Sentinel. It was the only way they'd find what they were longing to have.

"No more pain for you, sister," Sophie said emphatically as she floated toward the woman and put her palm on her upper back. The soul meant for Randolph entered the unhappy woman's body with a flash of light, her body jerking suddenly as she stopped crying.

Sophie smiled as she stood back and surveyed the situation, watching as the woman rose with a sense of determination and went to make herself something to eat.

"Eat well my new friend. You'll need the energy to deal with a Sentinel," Sophie warned the woman as she felt herself floating away, knowing that somehow Randolph would now find his mate. They'd encounter each other in the near future, and both of them would stop longing and start living for the first time.

*This is my special skill. This is what I'm supposed to do. I'm meant to help all of the Sentinels who lost their radiants find them again.*

Sophie was euphoric as she landed in Kristoff's bedroom. Maybe she couldn't bring back the exact mates that the Sentinels had lost, but she could bring back the *radiant* souls and meld them together with another woman who had been born to reincarnate the Sentinel mates.

The women she'd watched die hadn't ever really disappeared. Although their bodies hadn't been strong enough to endure, their souls had been kept safely to someday be reunited with their Sentinel.

As she solidified, she said joyously, "Best. Job. Ever."

"Sophie!" The anguished and angry voice of the Sentinel king roared out in the distance.

*I'm here. I'm at your house.* She sent the message out mentally to Kristoff immediately, sensing he was distressed. They'd been disconnected during the time she'd turned into some sort of phantom, losing her contact with her mate.

She waited, knowing he had to be frantic. If he had disappeared on her, she'd be devastated.

When she was in phantom form, her mind had disconnected with his, making it impossible to send him a message that she was okay.

When she was in the moment, she hadn't thought about it because what she'd been doing was so surreal that she simply followed her instincts.

Now, she realized that the disconnection had been painful, and she was exhausted.

Dizzy, she sat down on the bed.

"Where in the hell did you go!" Kristoff roared as he appeared in front of her.

She looked up at him, realizing with relief that their minds and bodies were connected again. Their bond hadn't been broken. It had just been temporarily blocked.

Sophie stood, looking at him with amazement. "I'm not sure you'll believe me. I'm not sure I quite believe it myself."

Kristoff took her by the shoulders and shook her gently, even though Sophie knew he was nearly out of his mind. "You scared the fucking hell out of me. Where were you, Sophie. What happened?"

She became dizzier and dizzier, and she slumped into Kristoff's chest. He caught her and held her against his strong, powerful body. His arms came around her protectively, holding her in a vise-like grip that Sophie couldn't have broken if she wanted to…which she didn't.

Even though what had occurred still seemed like a dream, she knew it was real. But it had taken a toll on her body.

With the energy she still had left, she told him simply, "I have a skill. It seems that I'm a matchmaker."

Kristoff began to shoot questions to her, but Sophie heard nothing more. Her world went black, but she wasn't worried. She'd never be scared again as long as her mate held her in his capable arms.

She let the darkness take her, knowing Kristoff would take care of her.

# Chapter Sixteen

Kristoff didn't let go of Sophie the entire night, nor did he sleep. He watched over his mate as she slept a healing sleep, discovering what had happened by sharing her memories.

*A matchmaker? How in the hell had that happened? She was more like a restorer of radiants.*

While he was grateful that his men would find their *radiants* like it was meant to be, he sure as hell didn't like the stress it put on his mate's body.

He watched the sunrise, the light filtering through the bedroom window as he held his entire life in his arms, wishing he could will her some of his strength. There was nothing he wouldn't give to keep Sophie from harm.

If this was her task, he couldn't keep her from doing what was in her power to do for his men. On the other hand, the thought of her drifting away from him again made him completely and unreasonably insane.

Her task would be never-ending. The soul of every *radiant* lost was in the small, soul-holding dimension. It wasn't just the women who died in the demon realm. Every *radiant* who died before meeting her mate from some tragedy had their soul on hold, waiting for Sophie. And there would be more. There had always been some

Sentinels who had never found their mate. Now that Sophie was here, it was her task to restore them all in the right women.

He was fucking conflicted. Never again did he want to feel disconnected from his mate. Yet his men deserved to be as happy as he was being bonded to his *radiant*.

"I can help." Athena's voice was unnaturally quiet as she approached the bed where he rested with Sophie.

He didn't take time for the niceties. "How? And how did you even know what happened?"

"I was called," Athena informed him sleepily, like she'd just gotten out of bed. "The oracles still speak to me occasionally."

"So you know what happened?"

She nodded.

"How in the hell do I make a decision between my men and my mate? My duty and my life? Damn the fates for giving Sophie this power but making her pay every time she does it. The souls are endless, Athena," he told the goddess huskily.

"I hold the remedy, Kristoff. You don't have to make that choice. You'll never have to make that choice. I didn't make you a king to have you tormented. You've waited a long time for Sophie. It's your time to be happy now." She moved forward and stood by the bed.

"What do I have to do?" he asked anxiously, ready to do whatever it took to keep his mate from feeling anything but joy in the future. "Sophie's had enough suffering."

Athena reached over and placed her hand gently on the top of Sophie's head. "You don't have to do anything. I'll give her what she needs to get through a reincarnation without losing contact with you, and without it being so hard on her physically. It's not my power. It's a gift I've always been holding for Sophie. I just never knew it until tonight." She paused and looked at Kristoff. "Giving her this gift will take away her scars, restore her to what she should have been. Are you okay with that?"

Kristoff really didn't want Athena to change a hair on Sophie's head, but if it meant that she could be stronger, powerful enough for them to stay connected and still do her job, he didn't care if her physical appearance changed.

Finally, he nodded at the hesitating goddess. "Do it. She sees her scars as ugly, so I doubt she'll mind. And they're a reminder every day to Zach about how he feels he failed her." He paused before adding, "I don't like seeing her changed at all. I love her. But I'll love her no matter what changes happen to her physical appearance. It doesn't matter. It never has."

Athena shot him a soft smile and quickly transferred her gift to Sophie without waking her up. As she pulled her hand away, she told him, "She'll still sleep for a while. But next time will be better."

"I sure as hell hope so," Kristoff rasped. "If it isn't, I'll lose my mind."

Athena rose up, shooting her brother a questioning look. "Does she know that you love her?"

She didn't. Not yet. But Kristoff knew he'd spill his guts pretty quickly when she recovered. There was no way he could hide anything from her for long.

"No," he answered simply.

"Tell her," Athena suggested. "I know from experience that a *radiant* needs to hear it. I think we get all hung up on the bond, but we want to be loved, too."

Kristoff wasn't quite sure how Sophie could *not* know how he felt, but since their joining didn't start off all that well, maybe she didn't. "She's everything to me, Athena. A miracle I never expected." He no longer felt like he needed to be guarded with his half-sister. In some ways, he'd always kept himself distant from everyone. Now, he wanted to be closer to his sister and get to know his daughter.

"I know," the goddess answered. "But it helps to hear the words."

"She'll hear them," Kristoff vowed.

Kristoff had never had the time to have a real discussion with Athena since she'd gotten freed by Hunter. "Are you really happy?" he asked curiously. "With Hunter?"

Athena sighed. "It could never have been with anyone but Hunter. He was always my protector, always sacrificing for me. I wish I would have known. I would have sent for him sooner. He went through a lot more pain than he needed to experience. When I asked you to send him to me, I still didn't know why. I just knew he held the key to something. I didn't know just how vital he was to my own happiness."

Kristoff regretted every punishment that Hunter had ever had to take for his behavior…now. At the time, he had been frustrated as he'd watched one of his friends sliding down a slippery slope that he was certain wasn't going to end well. "He can be an asshole," Kristoff warned her.

"Not anymore," Athena told him with humor in her voice. "Okay…yeah…maybe he is still a smartass, but he's a happy one. He's a good man. None of it was his fault. Kind of like you." She winked at him.

Kristoff was stunned by just how little anybody blamed him for what he used to be. "Do the rest of the Sentinels know?"

"What?"

"What I used to be. That we're related. That I was a killer."

Athena frowned at him. "Yes, they know. Before they went out to help search for Sophie, I thought it was better that they know everything. I wasn't sure at the time how any of it could be related, but I did give up your secrets. I'm sorry."

Kristoff shook his head. "Don't be sorry. Anything you ever do to better help protect my mate isn't an issue to me." He hesitated before asking, "What did they say?"

"The same thing everybody else would say. They respect you as their king, Kristoff. They always will. What happened before doesn't matter to any of them. What matters is who you are now. You've given and given for your men. All of them know you'd do anything for them. It's your turn now, brother. You've waited and suffered a long time for Sophie. Don't let your past destroy your future."

He could sense that Athena was about to leave, but he stopped her when he said quietly, "Thank you. I don't know if I've ever said that to you, or if I've ever told you that I love you. But since I've found Sophie, it seems more important than ever that you know how I feel."

"You have no reason to thank me. And I love you, too. You're my brother. I've always loved you."

Kristoff shook his head, amazed about how much Athena had changed. Once, she had guarded her emotions so well that they seemed not to exist. Now, she'd pour them out readily.

*She was much the same as I was once.*

"I'm thanking you for saving my life. Had I stayed with Zeus much longer, I'm not sure I could have ever come away with my sanity," he admitted honestly.

"I'm more than ready to let go of the past and the gods. There's very little they can do anymore. It's going to be up to the Sentinels to be the guardians of the world. Things will go back to as they were before our crisis, but the Evils will always be trying to rule the world."

"I think I'm up to the task," Kristoff told her with a grin.

"I know you are. I've always known." Athena smiled back at him.

Kristoff looked at the half-sister who had been a part of his life for so long that he couldn't remember when she wasn't. She was always his friend and confidante. Now maybe she could become more like a sister.

"You're a goddess, stronger than I am. I feel like you should lead us."

Athena shook her head. "I was never meant to be the Sentinel leader. A guardian, perhaps, but never a queen. That's her job now." She nodded toward the sleeping Sophie. "Since your bond with your mate, you're almost as powerful as I am. I gave up some of my power to save Hunter. I may have some skills you don't possess, but you were meant to be the Sentinel king." She hesitated before adding, "When I made you king, that role was irreversible. I can't create new Sentinels, I can't give them the power for the designations they will fulfill, and I can't take up your duties. Honestly, I don't want to, even if I could. If you don't mind, I'd just like to be Hunter's *radiant*. But like all of the Sentinels and their mates, I'll always watch your back."

He nodded slowly. "I am used to being the boss."

"I have what I want, and keeping Hunter in line is a big enough job for me. I'm tired, Kristoff. I'm ready to just be part of your team and a woman instead of a goddess."

Kristoff doubted he'd ever see Athena as anything *other* than a goddess, but since he was the only one who could be their leader, he was willing to let Athena be whatever she wanted to be. "Fair enough. You do need to keep Hunter in line."

Athena sighed happily. "It's not easy, but someone has to do it."

Kristoff knew it was a job that Athena relished. He could see the happy glow on her face. "Completely your job," he said jokingly. "I've tried to straighten him out for years and failed miserably."

Athena laughed. "I'm heading back home. Sleep well, brother."

His sister disappeared before his eyes.

"Kristoff?" Sophie mumbled and her eyes fluttered open.

Holding her tight against his body, he replied, "I'm here, love. Sleep."

"Is everything all right?" she asked sleepily.

She tilted her head to look at him and he swallowed hard as he saw the adoring look on her now unmarked face. Either way, Sophie looked the same.

She looked like she was his, and she always would be.

"Everything's good. Go back to sleep."

"My head feels funny," she answered with a grimace.

He passed a hand over her silken hair. "Do you remember what happened?"

She nodded slowly. "I'm a matchmaker." Her lips curled up and she beamed at him, blinking to keep her eyes open.

"You're more important than that. You're a *radiant* restorer. That's special." Actually, he got a kick out of how proud she was about being some kind of matchmaker, but the power to capture souls and bring together mates that otherwise would have never met was pretty impressive.

She nodded her head as her eyes drifted closed. "Best power ever," she said dreamily.

Seconds later, she was sleeping again. Kristoff kissed her forehead, his body screaming for him to fuck Sophie until they were both sated.

He ignored the temptation and held onto her tightly, just grateful to have her whole and happy in his arms.

Moments later, he slept without having a single nightmare about his past.

# Chapter Seventeen

ophie woke up slowly, the morning light coming from the bedroom window, beckoning her to open her eyes.

Even before she was entirely awake, her sense of well-being made her smile. Kristoff's powerful arms were around her, and she was sprawled over his gorgeous form, so warm and comfortable that she didn't want to move.

Blinking as she opened her eyes, she pushed herself up only to have Kristoff's grip on her unconsciously tighten as he slept.

She sighed, wondering if she'd ever get used to staring at her gorgeous mate. Rather than marring the perfection of his face, the stubble on his jaw just accentuated his masculine, sexy aura that had Sophie instantly craving him.

Smiling as she smoothed her hand down his body and slid to his side, it was no surprise when her hand finally encountered his silken, hard cock. It had already been pressed against her belly when she was waking.

Wiggling out of his grasp, she pushed back the covers and moved her hands over his chiseled body, but one of her hands kept returning to his erection. She was completely fascinated by the silken texture and the rock-hard surface beneath the soft skin and head.

There was a tiny bead of moisture on the tip, and she hungrily leaned over and swiped it off with her tongue. The taste was so tantalizing that she leaned down for more, sucking the upper portion of his cock into her mouth.

"You have about two seconds before you find yourself on your back with my dick buried so deeply inside you that we might never be separated again."

Kristoff's deep, dangerous voice startled Sophie.

*He's awake. He's been awake. I was just so consumed with him that I didn't notice that his mind was stirring.*

"My brain isn't the only thing stirring, sweetheart," he answered huskily, obviously picking up her thoughts.

Sophie let him slide from between her lips and turned her head until their eyes met. "Don't," she asked softly. "You know I've never really known a man before, and I want to see if I can make you feel as good as you make me feel. Please."

"Fuck! You're likely to kill me with pleasure. But I'll do my best," he said in a lazy baritone.

Sophie shared his mind, and she knew he wasn't as calm as he pretended to be. But she just wanted some time.

Once again, she sucked him between her lips, taking more of his cock this time, savoring his essence as she moaned her satisfaction of tasting him. She got greedier, and began to take as much of him as she could get.

Kristoff's hand gripped her hair, guiding her as he let out a long, tortured groan. "Christ, Sophie. That feels so damn good," he rasped harshly.

Encouraged by the fact that Kristoff found pleasure in her exploring his body, she moved her mouth up and down his rigid cock as his grip in her hair grew tighter, and more demanding.

"Off! Now!" Kristoff ordered in an urgent, demanding voice.

Sophie stopped and turned her head. She could feel his need, his body ready to spontaneously combust. Or was it her need? Oh hell, it was hard to tell anymore.

Climbing up his body, she positioned herself on top of him, her hand stroking him and she centered his cock exactly where she wanted it.

"Do it," he insisted, his voice hoarse with desire.

She lowered herself slowly, savoring every inch of Kristoff as she buried him inside her. "Oh, God. Kristoff. It feels so good, sometimes I don't know how to handle this."

"You've been handling *it* just fine," Kristoff answered, encouraging her.

"I can't get enough," she whimpered as she rose and lowered herself again.

Kristoff grunted as he grasped her ass and kept them joined, his cock buried to his balls. "Never enough," he agreed greedily, his hands caressing her ass.

White heat rocketed through her body as Kristoff slammed his hips up and thrust himself even deeper. "Yes," she hissed with satisfaction, letting her head fall back in ecstasy as Kristoff took over, pulling her down as he surged upward, his strokes so hard and deep that Sophie's body was shaking.

"Never enough," Kristoff growled again, his pace becoming impossibly brutal.

"More," Sophie gasped, needing his intensity like she needed her next breath.

"Touch your breasts, Sophie. Pleasure yourself. Take what you want."

Although she had no idea what to do, she followed the images Kristoff was forming in his head, seductive images of her pleasuring herself.

Obviously, the thought excited him, and as she touched her nipples, every sensation was heightened. She cupped her breasts, teasing the sensitive tips, then plucking at them harder and harder as Kristoff pummeled her with his cock. His eyes were raking over her upper body, his intense gaze watching both her face and her hands on her breasts.

"Too much," Sophie cried out. "I feel too much."

She was overwhelmed by the strength of Kristoff's thrusts, the feeling of having him deep inside her.

"It's not too much, love. Come for me, Sophie," Kristoff demanded as he gripped her ass even more tightly.

This was real, and it was intimate, the experience erotic and so sensually carnal that Sophie felt Kristoff in every part of her being. He permeated every nerve ending, exciting her to the point of madness.

Sophie felt her impending climax, her core clamping down on Kristoff's cock as her orgasm threatened to burn her alive.

"Kristoff, burn with me," she moaned, letting her hands fall to each side of his head as their eyes met and held.

"I already fucking do. Every damn moment since I met you," he told her as his chest heaved with desperation. "Kiss me, Sophie."

Her mouth was on his almost before he'd gotten out the words. She was no longer shy, no longer unsure of herself. Sophie gave herself permission to do anything she wanted, reach for what she needed. Invading his mouth with her tongue, she took ownership of her mate, just like he'd taken her. And damn, it felt so good. She devoured and tasted as Kristoff pushed back. When her mouth left his, she tongued the skin of his neck, then nipped his earlobe.

Raw need raced up as her climax slammed into her, and she screamed out his name as he continued to impale her with his cock.

Her climax reached its peak and as she saw his mating mark, she sank her teeth into the spot on his shoulder.

"Fuck!" Kristoff roared. "Yes. Mark me."

With his encouragement, she held onto his mark with her teeth as the muscles in her sheath reacted with spasm after spasm, milking Kristoff while he spilt himself deep inside her.

Letting go of his shoulder, she ran her tongue over the site where she'd bit him, noticing that there was barely a mark from where she'd attempted to brand him again.

In a heartbeat, Kristoff rolled and trapped her beneath him, his cock still deep inside her as he kissed her. His embrace was rough but loving, urgent, but the tender emotions were still there.

Wrapping her arms around him, she breathed in his masculine scent as he explored her mouth, then planted small, feather-light kisses on her face and her hair.

"Jesus! There isn't a single thing about you that doesn't move me, Sophie."

Her heartbeat had been slowing, but it hammered a couple of rapid beats as she felt the warmth of emotion spilling from Kristoff.

Gently, she tangled her hands in his hair and sighed. "I love you," she admitted quietly. "Maybe it isn't meant to be that way between Sentinel mates, but I love you so much."

He lifted his head and his eyes locked with hers. "I love you, too, baby. I always will. You're my life now, Sophie. And it's perfectly natural for mates to love each other. For me, it would be impossible *not* to love you."

Her eyes filled with tears as he said the words she thought she'd never hear from anyone except her brother. Kristoff was special, a man so compassionate yet so powerful that he took her breath away. Now that she shared his mind and thoughts, the two of them weren't so very different.

Both of them just wanted to be loved. They had been unconsciously searching for each other for a very long time, waiting.

Kristoff was so worth everything that had led up to her finally finding him.

Tears spilt from her eyes as she answered, "I couldn't not love you, either. Maybe my life was hell, almost literally, in the demon realm. But I'd do it all over again just to be with you."

"Ditto," he answered with a grin. "But you won't ever be doing anything bad over again, and neither will I. I think we've both waited long enough, sweetheart. It's our turn to be happy. I feel it. Don't you?" He kissed the tears from her face gently.

An acute wave of tenderness filled her as she answered, "Yes. It's definitely our time." The fact that Kristoff finally accepted that, and realized that he deserved to be happy made Sophie so overjoyed she spilled a few more tears.

And Kristoff was there to kiss them away. "I guess Athena was right," he observed after he'd kissed away the last drop of moisture on her face.

"About?" she asked curiously.

"It feels pretty damn amazing to hear that you love me. She said it would. And that you needed to hear how I felt about you, too."

"Hearing that you love me aloud is definitely good," she told him with a smile. "I feel it now, but hearing it is so much better. I guess because I've never really heard it before."

Kristoff was silent, his look thoughtful. "I don't think I ever did, either. Athena and I knew how to survive, but maybe we didn't know how to love or how to express it."

"She does love you," Sophie told him softly, stroking over his back with her fingers.

"I know. Probably as much as Zach loves you, even though you might never remember him actually saying it."

They were silent for a few moments, basking in the glow of being loved so deeply, and being certain that they'd always have each other's back.

When Kristoff moved off her to keep from squashing her, Sophie moaned softly. "My muscles hurt in places I didn't know they existed. I think I'll take a hot shower and see if it helps."

He smirked at her, knowing exactly where she hurt and why. "I'll come with you."

"You don't need to shower," she reminded him with a sultry smile.

"I do if you're there," he answered with humor in his voice.

Sophie was pretty sure he was up to mischief, but she was more than happy to play with him. Neither one of them had experienced much happiness. It was time to find out what it was like to do something just for the fun of it.

Kristoff was right behind her, and his large, naked body barely missed slamming into her as she stopped abruptly. "Oh, my God. My scars…" She was standing in front of the mirror on the dresser, unable to do anything but gape at her nude body and face.

"I forgot to tell you. Athena needed to deliver a jolt of power to you while you were sleeping. It will help you control your skill, and keep you from feeling the aftereffects as badly as you did yesterday. The only side effect from her doing that was it healed all of your scars." Kristoff grasped her shoulders from behind. "I hope you don't mind."

Sophie's eyes couldn't stop running over her face and her body. She was no beauty, but with her long dark hair and unmarked face, she was passable. "I'm almost pretty," she mumbled aloud.

"You're beautiful, baby. You always have been. You just couldn't see it," Kristoff told her gruffly. "Are you okay with how you look now?"

"Okay? Yeah. It's amazing." How could she ever thank Athena for what she'd done?

"You don't have to thank her. It's energy she's been holding for you for a very long time," Kristoff told her as he ran his hands up and down her arms.

"Are you happy with the way I look?" Sophie asked curiously.

Kristoff shrugged. "You look beautiful either way to me."

Sometimes his word flummoxed her, even though she knew it was true. He really *didn't* care, and it made no difference to him. "I'm glad they're gone, especially the demon marks. I've learned to live with them, but it feels like I'm starting fresh again."

"Zach will be happy, too. He's tortured himself forever about leaving you to die alone when you were sick. Maybe he can slowly forget and forgive himself."

"He will," Sophie said determinedly. "I'm so happy that I won't allow him to be anything less."

Kristoff let out a boom of laughter. "Then I know he'll forgive himself. It will be too hard for him to fight your spirit and your will."

"Am I so hard to resist?" she asked in a husky voice, her nipples hardening as her heart sang from seeing him laugh.

"For me? Impossible!" he confessed, his voice teasing.

"Then come with me," she suggested as she turned and wrapped her arms around the demon king that she loved with every part of her being.

He kissed her first, giving her a taste of the wicked seduction that was going to occur very shortly.

He took her hand and turned her around. "I'll come with you whenever you need me."

Sophie knew he was sexually teasing, but there was a vibration of truth in his tone and in his mind.

Kristoff would be there for her, and she'd be there for him. Although the whole mate situation was still surreal, she could get very used to it very quickly.

"Then I guess you'll be coming with me often," she said jokingly, shooting him a come-hither smile as she led him to the bathroom.

"Thank fuck for that," he answered in a low tone of relief.

She burst out laughing as she closed the bathroom door behind them, knowing that this was just the beginning. Kristoff was nearly done fighting his own demons, and beginning to find out what it was like to let go.

Sophie knew that life with the Sentinel king wouldn't always be easy, but she'd never done anything the easy way. The difference now was that Kristoff Agares, King of the Sentinel demons, was worth fighting for, and she'd help him exorcise any of his demons if they popped up in the future. And he'd do the same for her.

Let the bad things come and go. Their love would always be the victor.

After so many years of sadness, both of them were finally ready for love.

# Epilogue

*One Year Later…*

*I*t was a beautiful day for a barbecue.

Sophie watched as all of her and Kristoff's friends and relatives literally dropped in.

Zach and Kat entered first, teasing Sophie's husband as he cooked steaks on the grill. Since he didn't have to eat, it *was* rather amusing to see him grilling, and Sophie's brother immediately started giving his brother-in-law pointers, even though Zach was a terrible cook.

Kristoff could have just made the meal appear, but he was starting to enjoy doing human things, and Sophie enjoyed watching him do just about anything.

Really, she could just watch those powerful muscles ripple and his powerful movements all day.

Zach and Kristoff's relationship had become even tighter than it had been before, and Sophie loved Zach with all of her heart. She'd proved to him that he had no reason to feel guilty anymore, and he'd slowly stopped blaming himself for her fate as he'd watched her and Kristoff together. They were happy with their fate, which went a long way toward healing Zach's lingering pain over how she'd been taken by the Evils. And Kristoff…well…he gave Zach no reason to complain. He spoiled her terribly, and seemed to take pride in doing it. Neither his fierceness nor his tenderness ever stopped amazing her.

As Drew and Talia arrived and immediately joined in the friendly argument about the food, Sophie sighed. Drew clung to Talia's hand, his affection still just as obvious to anyone who saw them.

Athena and Hunter appeared last, and the group by the grill got louder. Hunter had changed, even during the last year. He'd mellowed out, his desire to slay demons slowly disappearing completely, much to his mate's relief. Not that he had done anything to require punishment like he used to do. But Athena had been afraid that the residual effects of him being an equalizer would make kicking the habit hard for her mate. If it had been difficult, Sophie had never noticed. All she'd seen was Hunter and Athena constantly supporting each other, even if they did argue on occasion.

Kristoff had gotten to know his daughter, Talia, and Sophie could sense a new closeness between father and daughter that had never had a chance to blossom in the past. Kristoff respected Drew as Talia's mate, but Sophie occasionally saw the Sentinel king watching his daughter and son-in-law protectively. But Drew still treated Talia like his own personal miracle, and Kristoff had never had cause to doubt Drew's love for his daughter.

Athena and Kristoff acted more like brother and sister now, with Athena constantly teasing her brother about something. It was heart wrenching to watch since they'd never had the chance to just enjoy each other's company. Now, they relished every minute of being siblings.

The goddess came in her direction, all of them taking a seat by her on the patio. "I think those fools are going to kill each other over steaks," Athena said with a happy sigh.

Sophie knew Athena would never allow one scratch on her mate, but the good-natured arguing between the men was common now, and she knew Athena wasn't really worried.

"Since Drew loves food, he might end up being the one to try the hardest to rescue the steaks," Talia added with smile.

"Zach's not really being reasonable, either," Kat added. "He just has to put in his two cents, even though he can't boil water without burning it. Honestly, Kristoff looks like he's doing an amazing job. He's changed so much."

Sophie looked at her brother's wife. "Is that good or bad?"

"Of course it's good," Kat said. "He never said so, but he was lonely."

Sophie supposed that was true. Kristoff had never shared much of himself, even with his friends. That had changed, and he'd spilled out his past to his friends, stunned when he realized that it made no difference to any of them. Not a single one had said a harsh word about what he'd done in the past. In fact, they'd all supported him, which had relieved Sophie's mind since she'd urged him to tell.

"How many matches has Queen Sophie done this week?" Kat asked jokingly.

"Only one," she admitted. "It's been a slow week."

She'd discovered that her power was only as good as the timing. Fate picked the time and the Sentinel who would finally get a mate. Sophie just made the arrangements.

Her power had become easy to handle with Athena's help. She'd matched up dozens of mates so far, and she cried with joy after every job. Eventually, she knew she'd bump into the Sentinel again with his mate.

Recently, she'd seen her very first case, Randolph, sporting his *radiant* on his arm. It had made Sophie happy to do something useful, and every case meant something to her.

She had a job she loved, a mate that loved her desperately, and friends like the women who sat around her, female confidantes that she could really trust.

Kat, Talia and Athena had helped Sophie adjust to being a *radiant*, which was so far from what she was used to that it had never stopped being surreal. Luckily, it was a time of peace on Earth, the Evils back to their normal strength, and the balance completely restored.

Still, that didn't mean that Kristoff was any less busy with his own duties. He still had bargains to oversee, problems to resolve, and carried the weight of the Sentinels on his very capable shoulders. He was an amazing leader and king, something Sophie never doubted he would be.

All of them had been grateful for the period of normality after the massively large imbalance that had almost destroyed the human realm. It had given them all time to experience some healing. Not that there weren't problems sometimes, because there always had been and always would be. But Kristoff handled his authority effortlessly, and managed his men just as well.

"Sweetheart…can you come be the judge on whether or not these steaks are done?" Kristoff bellowed to her.

She rose with a smile on her face, swaggering over to him in a pair of cutoff jeans and a tank top. "I'll look," she told her husband politely.

She picked up a knife and carefully slit one of the pieces of beef. It was perfect. "They look fine. Medium I'd say."

There was a friendly grumble from the other men, but her husband shot her a happy grin.

The food was spread on the table a short time later, and the men started to demolish everything, each of them making a plate for their wives before they started.

Sophie lingered on the patio, and Kristoff joined her.

"Aren't you coming to eat?" he asked with a frown.

"Shortly," she answered, smiling at him as he pulled her to her feet.

"There's a New York strip with your name on it," he teased.

"I love you," she blurted out, her eyes glued to Kristoff's handsome face.

"I love you, sweetheart." He put his arms around her so that she could rest her head on his shoulder. "Is everything okay?"

"Okay? No. Everything's perfect. Things are so good it's scary sometimes."

Everything that had happened seemed like her old life now, truly part of her past. This was her new life, and occasionally it scared the hell out of her to be so happy.

"You're afraid this will all end," Kristoff said huskily as he held her.

"Yes. I don't usually think about it. But today is so perfect with all of our friends and relatives here that it's hard not to think about it." She hated being morose, but once in a while she had to reflect on how much everything had changed in just over a year's time.

He rubbed her back. "It scares me sometimes, too."

The last thing she wanted to stir up inside Kristoff was uncertainty. Occasionally, they had disagreements, but it was usually about her safety. The Sentinel king was obsessed about her staying healthy and happy.

*Maybe because he sometimes feels the same way. Maybe sometimes he feels like all of this is too good to be true, too.*

"Sometimes I do," Kristoff answered in a soothing baritone, obviously catching her thoughts.

She let him hold her for a few minutes before she finally said, "I'm okay now. I'm sorry. Sometimes this whole life is overwhelming." Her moments of panic came less and less frequently, but once in a while the fear rose in her until Kristoff could dispel those insecurities.

She took his hand and started leading him to the table. "Let's eat. I hope they saved you something."

"If they didn't, they'll just claim it's because they were starving and I don't really need to eat," Kristoff grumbled, keeping a tight hold on her hand.

She turned and gave him a naughty smile. Over the last year, Sophie had learned just what it took to turn her husband on. Not that it really took much. "Are you coming?"

"You know I'd follow you anywhere," he answered.

"And if I walk into the house?" she challenged, her body clamoring for Kristoff as she sensed that he needed her, too.

"I'd definitely follow you there," he threatened.

She pulled on his hand. "Time to eat dinner," she reminded him.

"Only if I can have you for dessert," he retorted.

"Deal," she answered in a breathless voice, already envisioning what would happen later on.

"I'll have to sit through dinner hard as hell," he told her bluntly.

"I'll make it better later. I promise," she said with a laugh.

"I'll make sure you do," Kristoff said arrogantly. "Now eat. You'll need your strength."

She let Kristoff help her into a chair, her body starting to incinerate with every casual touch.

He took the seat beside her, teasing her while she consumed her steak, with images of what he had planned for *dessert*.

They might not have run out of their own party to go into their home so they could mess around while their friends and family were present, but it wasn't an easy temptation to resist.

She sent Kristoff a retaliatory mental image of what she wanted to do to him for dessert, and smiled as he reached for a glass of cold water.

They'd tease each other until they were half crazy while they were enjoying their barbecue.

But later…

Ah, later…

Sophie could hardly wait for *that*.

*~The End~*

Please visit me at:
http://www.authorjsscott.com
http://www.facebook.com/authorjsscott

You can write to me at
jsscott_author@hotmail.com

You can also tweet
@AuthorJSScott

Please sign up for my Newsletter for updates,
new releases and exclusive excerpts.

## Books by J. S. Scott:

*The Billionaire's Obsession Series:*
The Billionaire's Obsession
Heart Of The Billionaire
The Billionaire's Salvation
The Billionaire's Game
Billionaire Undone
Billionaire Unmasked
Billionaire Untamed
Billionaire Unbound
Billionaire Undaunted
Billionaire Unknown